SEND HER BACK

AND OTHER STORIES

SEND HER BACK

AND OTHER STORIES

MUNASHE KASEKE

MUKANA

Copyright ©2022 Munashe Kaseke
Published by Mukana Press
1200 Franklin Mall
Box 459
Santa Clara, CA, 95052
www.mukanapress.com

ISBN: Paperback: 978-0-578-35312-8
Hardcover: 978-0-578-32358-9
Epub: 978-0-578-32359-6
Audiobook: 9798218024895

Cataloging In Progress
Library of Congress Control Number (LCCN): 2022931814
Publication date July 2022

Book cover artwork by Patrick T. Gassaway

For immigrants
For women
For people of color

"Give me your tired, your poor,
Your huddled masses yearning to breathe free,
The wretched refuse of your teeming shore.
Send these, the homeless, tempest-tost to me,
I lift my lamp beside the golden door!"

Emma Lazarus 1883
Excerpt of poem at the base of the Statue of Liberty

CONTENTS

When Zimbabwe Fell
For Wyoming

He looked like a beautiful alien, with his translucent blue eyes that turned gray on cloudy days. When he wore his artichoke-colored hoodie that had clearly seen too many washes, they turned green. Each time we met, I gazed into them first, curious what color would stare back into mine. My boring dark brown eyes remained as loyal as the sunrise, held no surprises, and vowed allegiance to the state of their birth.

"I need some sun," he'd say, looking at his fluorescent white skin. I couldn't disagree more. It was his paleness that was most ravishing. When we held hands, our fingers interlocked; the pattern of alternating black and white digits was arresting. His skin always felt delicate, as though it were naked. I imagined that if you peeled my black coat off, I'd look like him underneath. I touched him with the utmost care, watching in fascination whenever it turned blue from a bruise, light peach after the sun's tan, or red and flaky after a burn.

"I'll never kiss a white girl again. Why date someone with bird lips when I can have all this?" he'd say and bite my lower lip. Closing my eyes, I felt his kisses in my stomach, in the hairs of my body, in my toes that carried my body weight as I stretched my neck to meet his lips.

I kept him entertained with stories of Shona culture. Everything from naked witches roaming the night to safari game drives at twilight. I promised to take him to stand before the mighty Victoria Falls, to show him the southern hemisphere sky, which, of course, is much prettier than the American sky. We talked on the phone for hours on end, late into witching hours, without a care for the responsibilities of the jobs that awaited us after the sun was born anew. I cooked him *sadza,* taught him to eat with his hands, made him kale sautéed in peanut butter, scrumptious beef curry stews, and introduced him to black Rooibos tea brewed with a dash of steamed milk and honey.

"Zimbabwean," he whispered after introducing me to his co-workers. He was an engineering manager at an autonomous vehicle Silicon Valley startup. "It sounds so exotic. When we get married, perhaps I can get a Zimbabwean passport and tell people I'm African American," he joked, squeezing my cold hand as we walked down Castro Street, its trees strewn in string lights creating a halo effect on the evening. I playfully shoved his hand away and rolled my eyes. He pulled me in and planted a kiss on my forehead. I smiled, placing a reciprocal kiss on his cheek.

"I can't believe you cook," he'd say. "In all my visions of a perfect woman, I never imagined that my future wife could cook. Who cooks in America in our generation?" I knew that just about everyone in Zimbabwe cooked; I wasn't that unique. I'd smile sheepishly as he took a bite, eyes shut, savoring every morsel, asking for seconds if any remained.

Four weeks after our first date, we were in proactive premarital counseling, emotions blossoming, the reinforced walls that guarded my heart crumbling. We hadn't decided on a ring yet. He believed diamonds were a scam.

"List things you don't like about each other, things that drive you crazy about the other person, big or small," the counselor said to all the giddy couples in the room. As the chatter swirled around us, we looked at each other bewildered, genuinely unable to come up with a single thing. We held hands, and his lips grazed my cheek. "We're going to have it so much easier than everyone else here," he said. I giggled in agreement.

He asked me to go to Wyoming to meet his family over Memorial Day weekend. It was ninety degrees. I struggled to remember their names, the skinny redhead in an overflowing blue dress with eyes that matched his on a sunny day. The ever-smiling, almost identical blondes, save for the fact that one had curly hair, the other straight. The buff older brothers in checkered shirts, their wives. The spirited toddlers running around. The large black dog that wouldn't stop licking my toes. The family friend. The parents.

Faded photographs hung on the walls, displaying younger, happier versions of themselves. I noticed a sibling in all the pictures was missing on this day.

After a day of people coming in and out and the unbearable humidity that caused my pores to cry and my hair to rebel, I was disoriented.

"A work emergency came up," he announced, entering the living room. "I need to fly back to California." I quietly let out a sigh of relief.

He turned to me and looked me in the eyes. "But maybe you stay so my family can get to know you better?" My eyes grew wide. Excitement filled the room, a chorus "please" drawn out for effect. I shut my mouth, which I realized was hanging open, swallowed hard, and nodded.

After he left, I sat in the living room, surrounded by ten sets of eyes. *Will you settle in Zimbabwe after you get married? I want to have a relationship with my grandkids—you can't move there. Did you know he went through a depression not too long ago? Do you know he doesn't want a big wedding, he'll probably make you elope? Do you know he hates scents? Don't wear perfume around him. He's incredibly close with a female friend who has lived with us for the last five years. She's a single mom, and he's a father figure to her daughter, buys her books and kites all the time.*

As the questions rained, my heart began rebuilding the walls that had crumbled so easily. Who was this man? I didn't have the answers to most of their questions.

He picked me up from the airport, excited. "I was reading something about Shona culture, and I learned a new word today," he said. Though frazzled by his family's interrogation, when I was met with hazel eyes, a hue I'd yet to see, I left my trepidation at the airport. With eyes like that, we could work through anything. My heart shimmied, amazed at how keen he was to learn my tongue. We drove down Highway 280, undulating green hills dotted with large, envy-evoking homes peeking through the trees on one side, the Coastal Mountain Range, with fog crowning its peaks, and Upper Crystal Springs Reservoir shimmering in the tangerine sunset on the other. He grabbed my hand and placed it on his thigh, where it sat until we arrived at my place.

Roora was the word he'd learned in my absence.

"I get to *buy* you from your family! How much do you think you're worth?" he asked nejinja, excited.

"You're not quite *buying* me," I explained. "It's a gift of gratitude that you give to my family. Kind of the same way a man here buys an expensive engagement ring for his fiancé. It's just that instead of the expensive gift coming to me and sitting on my finger, it goes to my family."

He laughed. "Spin it however you wish—I'm *buying* your ass," he said as he kissed my lips. I looked into his now gray eyes and smiled, shaking my head as I felt my bones echo from his touch.

That evening, I lay my head on his chest with its fine silky hairs, some blond, some brown, others even red. He stroked my black curls as I listened to his heartbeat. Determined to uproot the seeds of apprehension, I began unraveling the scroll of questions that had been presented to me in Wyoming.

"Kids?" I asked.

"It's a big deal to bring a soul into the world. That's something we can discuss after we're married."

"Money?"

I learned that he had bad credit and fifty-five thousand dollars in college debt, which he'd stopped repaying, he hadn't filed his taxes in two years, and he'd "invested" thirty thousand dollars, his life savings, in a political betting site.

It's not that I wanted kids or was against marrying anyone with debt, though I had none. It's just that I had grown up seeing poverty first-hand. To me, life was never kind; you had to fight in life to stand a chance. In my world, you figured out what life should look like ten years beforehand so you could attempt to prepare for its cruelty. His nonchalant, *we'll figure everything out as it happens* approach terrified me, struck me as irresponsible, especially for someone eight years older. Never mind that I had come to the US alone in my early twenties, yet I suddenly seemed to be lightyears ahead of him.

"I like that you're not the regular kind of black," he announced two weeks later. "African Americans are never objective. They won't consider the facts about police shootings, for example."

Then, "I'm not a feminist. They're crazy."

Three months later, I could write a book about the things I didn't like about him. That artichoke hoodie that turned his eyes green was too dilapidated. He stopped taking me out to eat, saying that he preferred my cooking. I felt like a Netflix and chill girl. I hated that he watched shows with so much nudity and sex without flinching. Having been raised in conservative Zimbabwean circles,

I couldn't believe it would be okay for husbands to stare at other women's naked bodies, even if they were acting out a story. Plus, he didn't worship; he told my deeply spiritual self. I found myself constantly thinking, "uyu ndiwo unonzi muyedzo, mashiripiti chaiwo." – The relationship felt like a cruel joke. As though someone was researching my fondest pet peeves and constantly feeding him lines.

"When do I get to meet your family?" he asked. In my culture, parents meet a boyfriend on the day of roora. Before that, they don't even want to hear as much as a suggestion of dating. I tried to explain this, but he thought I was equivocating.

"Well, then give me a roora date," he demanded. I couldn't, unsure I wanted to marry him.

We fought, doors banged, phone numbers blocked, Instagram accounts unfollowed. Then I received an email detailing his undying love for me, describing all the things that made him giddy when he first met me, reminding me of how intoxicating we'd found each other to be. He reminded me that all couples fight; we could get through this if we didn't give up. A few hours later, there was a knock on my door. Dark blue eyes that matched his shirt stared back at me. Everything I'd felt in our early days flooded back. I rushed into my beautiful alien's arms. We kissed until we cried.

I was ready to work it all out that evening, leave with a twelve-step plan on how we were going to resolve everything. I suggested we go out to eat at a nice restaurant in Santana Row.

"May you cook instead? Let's stay in and find something to watch." he countered, flipping through the channels. He paused on a news station. "I hate these liberals, calling themselves progressives," he asserted.

"Can we go somewhere and spend time talking about our issues instead of society's ills?" I replied, ignoring his words but not the feeling of his left hand caressing my thigh.

"It's too exhausting. Not everything needs to be planned," he replied as he continued flipping.

Mukomana wacho aiita kunge chirahwe - I couldn't tell, was he a jerk or simply American? Frustration welled up within me again, and within a few weeks, the cycle began anew. Blocked numbers, passionate apologetic emails, knocks on my door, kisses, and repeat; round and round, for two years. I finally told him to never come to my door again, or I'd call the police. I stopped responding to his emails, marked them as spam. It's been five months since the last one. Every morning, the first thing I do is check my spam, but all I get are notifications of money I just won.

Send Her Back

I pull to the side of the road, peering into my rearview mirror, and hold my breath. No sudden movements, I remind myself. Hues of blue flash in the dark, red alternates. A loud ring accompanies the lights as they draw closer. I squeeze my steering wheel, the assault on my ears ceases, and the lights rest behind me. A pale white officer, his skin a blunt contrast to mine, approaches. I turn my head, and our eyes lock.

Agitated, he knocks on the window, gesturing for me to roll it down. I blink out of my stupor, obeying with a quivering hand. I should've known to do this without command. He asks for my license. I request permission to look in my glove compartment. Following a nod, papers scatter, middle compartments open, my eyes itch, and I clench my teeth. I know it's not there; I don't have a license, yet search I continue, murmuring a prayer under my breath.

"What's your name?" the officer's voice pierces through the suburban silence.

"Vimbiso Nyamukundwa."

He raises his eyebrows, frowns, then shakes his head as if to say that's not acceptable.

"Where are you going this late?"

I'm on my way back home from work at the nursing home, but if I tell him I have a job, I might end up with two infractions; I'm not supposed to hold a job. I pause in silence. He gapes at me with large bulging eyes, and I notice a large black mole on his left cheek. I could swear I've seen him before.

"I...I'm not up to anything. I'm just...just driving," I stutter, quickly glancing at the time on the dashboard - 12:34am.

He laughs.

He takes a few steps back towards his fellow officer, positioned by the trunk of my car.

"I bet she's from one of them shit holes," the questioning officer says to his counterpart.

He walks back to me and asks where I am from.

"Zimbabwe," I respond shakily. In my head, I think, Ndaibva. Yafira pano – I'm done for.

He winks at his mate. "Can I see your papers?" he asks with a satisfied grin.

My stomach ties itself into a lasso. I gulp and tell him that I don't have them with me. He signals to his friend, and I stare at the badge on his chest that has long been the subject of my nightmares.

"You'll have to come with us," he says.

He opens the driver's door and orders me out. I rise, my hands in the air. My face slams onto the car roof; his hand on my neck is too tight; I flinch. The officer orders me to put my hands behind my back; I don't, too stunned to move. He shoves them down and cuffs my wrists; the metal is ice cold.

"Move, shit hole!" he says as he drags me into their car.

"Call Karl, tell him I picked up another one for him. He'll need to come to the station right away. I can't hold her for long," he says to his colleague.

The seat is comfortable, but its black leather sends chills down my toes. A steel wire fence separates me from the officers in the front. I've imagined this scene countless times over the last nine years. Finally, a physical representation of my caged existence has manifested. Streetlights perforate the dark of night. I can't go back; things were starting to come together; I'd finally been accepted into medical school. I must fight. I listen to the officers' excited chatter about helping ICE clean up the town as we speed off.

• • •

A WEEK AFTER THE ARREST, my lawyer pays me a visit, or at least that's what Esi says he is. He is so tall that he needs to lower his head to enter my apartment. He removes his maroon leather shoes with tiny holes on the pointed tip, placing them next to my well-worn sneakers and sandals. Walking past my open-plan kitchen, he stretches himself out on the single brown couch in the living room; his gray elbows are a clear sign that he has neglected to apply lotion. It reminds me of my Munya and I'm strangely comforted by it. My eyes fixate on the tear on the armrest. I meant to mend it after picking it up from the street but never got around to it. As the lawyer rests his arm over it, I'm ashamed of its shoddiness.

After the arrest, I was met by two ICE officers at the police station. I was charged with being deportable, and a bond was set. Esi, my Ghanaian roommate, paid it as soon as she found out. A Notice To Appear (NTA) was handed to me three days later, and a court date (Master Calendar Hearing) was scheduled two weeks out.

"You shouldn't have said anything! They can't detain you," Esi had lectured.

" And why were you being a saint? It's just a job! Your shift doesn't end that late. Now, if it were me, that woman would suffer, I tell you. I get deported because of her? Oh God help her!" she said, pacing up and down the room, flicking her fingers above her head.

A resident had slipped, injuring her pelvis. She became anxious and delirious, so I stayed longer to calm her, and now I was paying for it. I shake my head.

"That's not helpful, Esi. It doesn't change what happened. Besides, nobody forced me to stay," I responded.

Esi always had an opinion about everything I did or did not do, much to my appreciation. When I couldn't figure out how I was going to get a job after coming to the US on a tourist visa, she arranged the job at the nursing home, assuring me they would pay me in cash because much of the town's population was aging, yet all the young adults were leaving for Dallas or Austin, for flashier jobs where they fiddled on computers all day, for late nights in bars, drinking colorful cocktails and bobbing their heads to rap and house music. Where they could attend live theater shows or try Thai food. In this town, Esi had assured me, they just needed young people willing to do all the manual labor jobs that their own youth eschewed.

It was Esi who invited me to move in with her, splitting rent so I wouldn't have to put my name on the lease or pay the full price of an apartment. It was Esi who supported my dream to apply to medical school, suggesting that I request a transcript of my University of Zimbabwe Biology degree. After all, Zimbabwe's education system was modeled after the British as a former colony, making it easier for American schools to understand the credit conversion. It was Esi who "covered" my shifts at work while I spent long days at the library studying for my MCATs, assuring me that the old people at that home wouldn't know the difference between two Black, African women. It was Esi who told me that there was no federal law that prohibits the admission of undocumented immigrants to US universities; I could use my Zimbabwean passport and birth certificate. Some states even allow undocumented students to pay in-state tuition rates under certain conditions. And though I didn't know how I was going to afford California rent, let alone the full cost of medical school, with Esi whispering in my ear, nothing felt impossible.

I'm startled by the lawyer's cough. I face him eagerly.

"I've done this many times for people from all over the world," he assures me, mistaking the shame my face carries for consternation over my deportation case. "No need to worry." From his thick accent, I can tell he is West African, though I cannot place his exact country of origin. Knowing that he's a black African immigrant like me eases my fear.

I grab the pen and paper I had set on my kitchen counter in anticipation of his visit and sit on the floor. "It's going to cost three thousand dollars," he says with a straight face.

At that, I squint and fold my fingers into fists, digging my nails into the palms of my hands nervously. I can't afford that. He reads the expression on my face correctly this time. I consider appealing to him like a brother. If any lawyer is going to sympathize with me, it's this guy. Do I begin by telling him how much I make and how hard I work, or do I lead with the desperate state of my country? I open my mouth, but before I can get the first word out, he speaks.

"I can leave if that's too expensive for you," he says as he lifts himself from the couch. "I have a family to feed as well."

"No. It's no problem," I lie. "I will work extra shifts, earn some overtime, find extra work," I add, more to reassure myself than him. A sense of betrayal sweeps over me; isn't he too an African immigrant?

He stares me down, then reclaims his seat. Chewing on my pen, I ask him what I'll need to get started. He asks for my MDC membership card.

I shake my head, confused. The MDC is the main opposition party to the ruling ZANU-PF in Zimbabwe. I am not a member of either.

"You need to apply for asylum. This way, your case will be adjourned for an individual hearing, a full hearing. The judge schedules only a few cases a day for individual hearings, which buys us time. We need to convince USCIS that your life and your husband's are in danger from ZANU thugs because you're an activist who have been denouncing the ruling regime. We need proof you are MDC."

I sense hope rising once more. I'm sure I can pay someone in Zimbabwe to get me a membership card. I smile at his genius and repeatedly nod as I fail to find my words.

"Your husband is in Zimbabwe, right? Hire someone to knock a few of his teeth out, give him a stern beating, break something. Have him go to a hospital in Harare and get medical records detailing the trauma. Get some pictures of his injuries, too, and send all this to me," he says as he casually wipes off a drop of sweat that sprouts on his forehead.

I laugh but quickly realize he is serious. Watching new sweat drops form on his forehead, I apologize for not having air conditioning in this Texas heat.

"Is there any other way?" I ask as fear and hopelessness creep back in. He hushes me, refuting the unspoken objections he knows I have to the details of his plan. As he chatters on about why this is the most effective way, I can tell that he certainly has done this before.

"I need the documents and a fifty percent down payment by Friday," he says as he makes his way to the door. "You don't have much time to appeal."

As he walks out, I close my eyes and count the days till Friday. *Five*, I say to myself and take a deep breath, staring at the phone that has become synonymous with my husband. Nowadays, when I think of Munya, I no longer see his face, or recall his scent, or how the caress of fingers feels—no, when I think of him, I see my white iPhone 5 with its cracked screen. How can I ask this of him?

I left Zimbabwe at age thirty, a university graduate who had been working as a secondary school teacher in Bulawayo for five years. Munya and I were married for a year when I left, delirious for each other, with dreams of big jobs, a big home, a big family, big paychecks, big vacations, big...happiness. We were smart, hardworking and all we needed was a chance, a fully functioning economy to pour our youthful years into. Our determination, zeal, and discipline would make us effortlessly rise in comparison to our peers. With Zimbabwe ailing, our government paychecks had begun to dwindle until they stopped coming entirely despite us still being expected to show up and teach. It was at this point that we decided our dreams would fizzle and be buried in the graveyard of our economy. We were better than that; we weren't just going to take it! I would move to the US, find a well-paying job in a lab somewhere, put my experience to good use, then sponsor Munya to follow a year later, but the US immigration system scoffed. And with each year that passed after my tourist visa expired, rendering me undocumented, our hopes shrank; we found a new type of dream graveyard.

By Wednesday, I've gathered enough courage to call Munya. He answers on my fifth attempt, prevented from doing so sooner by the fact that I kept hanging up after the first ring. I fiddle with the letter in my hand, and take in the voices of his neighbor's young children chattering on his end. "I will be able to bring you here soon. Someday we can have our own," I explain without prompting, swallowing back the guilt. It's never far from my mind that I just celebrated my thirty-ninth birthday, and the window for me to give my husband's offspring a legacy to carry his name is closing.

"No hurry, my wife, I understand," he responds calmly. "It's better you stay in America and work; send money for us to finish building our own home. I'm trying, but it's hard."

Munya hasn't been able to hold a job since being laid off from his administrative job at Lever Brothers in 2010 which he got after we left our teaching jobs. Zimbabwe's unemployment and inflation continue to soar. I can't go back. Not only does Munya rely on me, but his parents, his siblings, my parents, my siblings, my grandmother, and my nieces also depend on me for groceries, clothes, and school fees. Not only that, I contemplated ndinonyarirepi – what will people say?

I appreciate his patience with me. Though it's been nine years since we've seen each other, he never pushes me to return home as other men whose wives sought refuge overseas do. Our arrangement thus far has worked. Though I haven't been able to give him the son he'd always wanted after my miscarriage back in Harare in 2010, he patiently awaits our reunion. At times, I wonder if he is so patient because he already has a *smallhouse* and with whom he perhaps has secret primary school-aged children, and the money I'm sending is truly for his *smallhouse's* makeup and latest fashion and the children he would never confess to fathering with her.

"Mudiwa, I received a deportation order a few days ago," I say as I stare at the notes I took when I met with my lawyer. In the center of the page, "$3000" is inscribed in large letters. I circled it four times and underlined it twice. I have traced each character over and over again in dark blue ink; the ink is leaking onto the back of the page, the paper almost torn along the characters.

Munya's voice sinks, rife with concern. We sit in silence. The kettle I had set on the stove for tea starts to whistle, startling me. I rush to pick it up but tip it over, scorching my hand. I groan and tell Munya that I just gravely burned myself.

"No! You cannot return! What about my money?" he says with a loud yet shattering voice.

Did he hear what I just told him about my hand? Is there no concern for my well-being? Does he think I want to return empty-handed? Give up a decade of life lost toiling in the US for the sake of our future? Does he care about my emotional state at all?

The burden his voice carries is stifling. It sounds like a burden for his welfare, not mine. Though he doesn't say it, I know he is worried that without my monthly remittances, there is no hope for a blissful future. I wonder if US dollar bills are all he sees now when he tries to picture me, or perhaps a Western Union logo. Annoyed by his lack of concern, I find the courage to share the lawyer's request.

"I can apply for asylum. If I can make a case that I was a member of the MDC and it's politically dangerous for me to come back, I might stand a chance to stay. If I'm granted asylum, then you too could join me."

He doesn't respond. I know that he, like me, is not sure that any of this will work. We had previously tried to have him apply for a visa to study in the US, but his application was denied because I am undocumented.

"You... You will need to hire some people to beat you up, break something, knock out a few front teeth, then report to the hospital that you were assaulted and get some medical records for proof," I continue, my hand searing, the rest of me completely numb. You would...."

His voice bursts through the phone, a baritone that seems foreign, from a distant memory. "Now you have lost your mind, woman! You think because you make more money than me, you can tell me what to do? Nonsense! If you want me to move on, just say so. If you want to find a reason to move on, just do so! Don't get me murdered in the name of papers. What kind of witchcraft are you practicing now that requires the teeth of a husband as an ingredient? I have been quiet all these years—but I know you could've been sending more money. You're living the high life over there. I see you in a different fancy outfit each time you send a picture. I see you getting fat, those cheeks blowing up over the years of good living. I hear you whisper when I call you, and you're at work. You're hiding me because you're ashamed. You lie and say you want my children when you will be barren soon. Vimbiso, you take me for a fool, promising I will come soon, yet you said you're starting school again..."

I drop my phone as he lets the deluge of everything he has wanted to say over the last decade out. The frustration he has felt, the anger wrapped in niceties, oozes out. I sense an odd sense of relief.

The guilt I've carried, the shame, the frustration I've wanted him to express is finally here. We are having a real conversation, laying bare our true emotions. I sense him again, not the shell of a human I've been interacting with for years. Not the puppet that simply says please and thank you to conversations revolving around how many U.S. dollars are needed. For the first time in almost a decade, I sense the passion in him, an awakening. Perhaps there's a chance that our love can return.

I gasp for air, realizing I had neglected to breathe. I feel dizzy and hang up, turn my phone off, pretending my battery is dead.

• • •

"LEAVE HIM! IT'S BEEN too long. Besides, you need to be saving for Cali," Esi shouts when I tell her about our conversation. But before getting accepted into medical school, I felt like I was failing at everything. See, my life at thirty-nine looks nothing like I dreamed it would. Everything feels fickle, my world rickety, my identity shifting, ever so capricious. Something about still being married, still trying to make it work, despite the distance and challenges, makes me feel like I'm still "winning" at something. This is the *one* thing on the "Vimbiso At Forty" vision board that I crafted right before leaving for the US that holds true, and forty is seventeen days away. Perhaps a "Vimbiso At Forty-One", living in California, and a physician in training, might make a different choice.

I know after my conversation with Munya that asylum isn't an option. In frail optimism, I tell myself that there is another way. I will find a way to remain in the US; my work will not be in vain. I will find a way to bring my husband to join me. I will find a way to feed my family. Perhaps I can convince the US government that I am otherwise a law-abiding citizen. I work hard caring for its citizens—their parents and grandparents, their veterans, and the sick. Each day I bathe the residents, change diapers, feed them, and offer conversation and company when their own kids are too busy with their lives to care. I am the residents' constant companion until their families can schedule an hour over the weekend to visit with fake smiles and patronizing loud voices as if the residents can't be understood. I see them in condescending voices, lecturing their elders as though wisdom diminishes with age. If only they took as much time as I did to be invested. Do you want to know about a people? Watch how they treat the vulnerable, if they care nothing for their own blood, locking them up in homes because they are too busy for their own mother and father, what then do you expect them to do with a stranger, a foreigner like me, with skin this black?

I retreat to my room, take a nap and wake up feeling more rested, hopeful, and ready to consider the possibility of continuing my journey. I lift the large white envelope on the kitchen counter and read my medical school acceptance letter once more. I will figure this out. If the American people knew my sacrifices, how smart I am, how I'm going to be the best cardiologist there ever was, and how I'm willing to work in remote rural towns where they are in need of specialists, surely, they would be merciful. They would understand. As the sun sinks beyond the horizon that evening, I pick up my phone and fidget with it. I turn to the Twitter app for distraction. The first video I see is of a formidable white crowd chanting, "Send Her Back! Send Her Back!" The face of a woman, black like me, comes up. I read she's from the same continent as me; she's an American citizen now, a congresswoman. Instantly, I feel a pounding on my head, right above my left temple. I feel as though I've just been dipped in a bucket of ice water. If she's not accepted, not welcome, what hope do I have? I should stop watching and put my phone away, yet I follow the rabbit hole to President Donald Trump's page. My scrolling leads me to a tweet he posted four weeks ago.

"Next week, ICE will begin the process of removing the millions of illegal aliens who have illicitly found their way into the United States..."

The tears I have fought since the arrest flood my cheeks. Lowering myself to the floor, I wrap myself in the fetal position and sob myself to sleep, the acceptance letter clutched on my bosom.

• • •

A LOUD KNOCK LANDS on my door. I jump in fright.

"There's no time to recoil, sis. It'll be fine. Chin up. Go get that paper!" Esi yells as she leaves for work.

I want to scream that she's wrong this time but instead decide that if I'm going to return, I may as well not be empty-handed, so I get up and ready myself for work.

Mrs. Jones is the first resident I'm scheduled to bathe and feed. I have developed an aversion toward her. Her pelvis and anxiety cost me my future. Her grandchildren are scheduled to visit. I wheel her into the lobby, recalling Esi's words about retribution if my case is denied. The wheelchair squeaks on the maple floors. I shake off the thought. I'm better than that.

In the lobby is a man with bulging eyes and a large black mole on his left cheek standing with the grandchildren. I gasp. The cop! They can't be here to get me already; what about the Master Calendar Hearing? He tilts his head, raises his eyebrows, frowns then shakes his head.

 Three children, all no older than six, rush toward us and embrace Mrs. Jones. The youngest, confused, lifts her arms, gesturing for me to pick her up. I'm not sure what to do. She begins to cry, and her older brother tells me that she likes being held. Keeping my eyes on the cop, I slowly lift the child, my heart racing.

The cop shifts uncomfortably, his gaze unrelenting.

"No hugs from you, my son?" Mrs. Jones says to him. He pauses, then slowly walks over, planting a kiss on her cheek.

"I was going to leave the kids but.... It's an emergency! I need to return at the end of the day but... " he says as he tinkers nervously with the set of keys in his jean pocket.

"Hurry along. We're in great hands with Vimbiso over here,"

Mrs. Jones says as she reaches for my hand.

He stares at his youngest in my arms, her head resting comfortably on my shit hole shoulder.

Return To The Land
Of Giant Suns

The people on the planes became Blacker and Blacker with each layover. On the North Dakota to Washington D.C. flight, I was the only Black person, as was usual in most places I frequented in North Dakota. Then from Washington D.C. to London, there were a handful of us. London to Johannesburg, half the flight was Black and from Johannesburg to Harare, there was one white person. I watched from my window seat as the miniature buildings and cars below us became larger, more life-size as we finally descended into Harare. I smiled at the flight attendant's Shona announcement of our arrival. I hadn't heard a word of my tongue in a public space for five years. Finally, I was home, a place I fit in entirely.

After we deplaned, I stood in the line for Zimbabwean citizens that circled around the corner. The foreigners' line had only one person, who was promptly served. I felt a little annoyed. Anytime I'd traveled to other countries, the foreigners' line was the one that wound while citizens received the red carpet, hassle-free entry. When I reached the front of the line, the agent asked for my name. She wore an army green uniform and had soft, kind eyes. Her wide lips were smothered in an almost orange lipstick that stained two of her front teeth. M-A-K-A, I began to spell, then remembered, I was no longer in North Dakota. I interrupted myself and smiled. "Makanaka Mutusadonha," I said instead. She promptly wrote it down, asked where I lived, in my native Shona tongue, then followed up with questions about life in the United States. I eagerly answered, enjoying the way my tongue curled as I spoke, making sounds I had almost forgotten I knew how to make.

She remarked that three weeks was too short a visit for someone who hadn't been home for half a decade, then scornfully added, "No wonder you have a hard time with Shona."

I looked at her bewildered. We were chatting in Shona, weren't we? My responses had been perfect, my grammar sublime. What did she mean I had a hard time with my language?

"Your accent is funny. The way you pronounce some words tells everyone you don't live here."

My heart sank to my stomach.

She stamped my green passport, then motioned for the next person in line before I could respond.

As I exited the terminal, I was met with giddy faces. My parents, my older sister, and her husband plus their two children—nephews aged five and three I'd never met. Their embraces cuddled my soul. The exhilaration of seeing family faces for the first time in half a decade overwhelmed me. They all looked a lot older, as though I had been gone for fifteen years, not five. Half my mother's hair was white, my father had a slight wobble when he walked, and their wrinkles shouted for attention. Their weary eyes seemed to have sunk deeper into their skulls. My brother-in-law was clad in a navy-blue suit, a white shirt, and a maroon tie. His leather shoes reflected the glare of the setting sun. A smell like that of freshly plucked chickens filled the air. I inhaled it and smiled.

"Is this how someone coming from America dresses?" my brother-in-law mocked, looking at my sweatpants and hoodie.

I needed to be comfortable for the gruesome journey. Besides, I had left North Dakota thirty-eight hours ago and had not showered since, nor had I gotten any sleep. I tried explaining but to no avail.

"You need to dress better. Are you homeless out there? And your complexion, still as dark ever. Kuita tsito kudai? The snow didn't change you, huh?" he carried on.

I turned my attention to the kids instead and asked for their names in Shona. They stared blankly at me then looked up to their mother for guidance. I supposed they were shy, I was, after all, a stranger, the aunt they knew only from pictures.

"They don't understand Shona, speak to them in English," my sister instructed me.

I laughed, but soon realized she was serious. A cloud of sadness drizzled over me. How could children born and raised in Zimbabwe, who didn't even have passports fail to speak our mother tongue?

We packed my three suitcases into the trunk of the car, my parents sat in the front, and the rest of us squeezed into the back seat. The five-year-old, Jayden, was instructed by her mother to sit on the middle compartment with his back toward the windshield. The younger one sat on his mother's lap. My eyes widened. Car seats anyone? If we braked suddenly, Jayden would fly right through that windshield. I decided to start the visit on a good note and remained quiet. I would bring it up later. I reached into my purse and picked out two teddy bears for each of my niece and nephew.

"It's a bheya!" Jayden said with a smile that showed his almost toothless mouth.

"Say *bear*," I responded, pulling the toy back to my chest. My sister eyed me disapprovingly.

"If they're going to speak only one language, they better speak it well," I said unapologetically.

As we drove home, the sun retreated entirely, ushering in an eerie darkness. Streetlights lined the road leading from the airport, like well-arranged fireflies. Each light pole had a small solar panel above it. I remarked that I was impressed the city was going green and finding ways to keep the city alight despite the power cuts I had read about.

"We'll see how long it lasts. They tried that with the robots that direct the traffic, but the solar panels were stolen overnight," my father said.

I shook my head in disbelief. We hit a pothole as we exited the main highway into the suburbs, and I reached out to steady Jayden. My mother laughed, "You're going to try to do that the entire way home? He's fine," she said.

As we left the highway, the potholes seemed to get worse. In the dim of the night, the road appeared so worn out, it was now a dirt road with a few patches of tar sprinkled unevenly across. I watched the rusted buildings that lined the street. They clearly had not seen a fresh coat of paint in decades. I stared in fascination and depression as we made our way home. It was not just my family that looked like they had aged fifteen years, my whole city looked like it had been an abandoned ghost town for two decades and everyone just moved back in yesterday and were trying to fool me into thinking that they had been here all along.

A young woman with a baby who was no older than a year stood begging in the middle of the street at a traffic light that did not work. On the side of the road was another beggar with outstretched arms, blind with a white cane, tattered clothes, and bare feet. I turned my gaze back to the shivering baby and my heart moved. It was so easy for me to ignore beggars without a flinch of guilt in North Dakota, but these were my people. I reached into my bag to see if I had loose change. My father promptly rolled up the car windows and hissed at the woman and her child not to approach. I looked up in surprise.

"Street kids! They are a bunch of brutes without manners. Be careful to keep your car windows up, they could snatch your purse," he said.

I felt bad for judging him, after all, that was how I reacted to the homeless in the US. If memory served me right, I used to roll up my windows when beggars and street kids approached me in Harare as well before I left for the US.

When we arrived in Greendale, I gave the three suitcases to my family. They were filled with clothes, chocolate, perfume, Walmart electric toothbrushes, and toys for the kids. They opened each suitcase and divided the spoils among themselves. I reminded them that the chocolate and perfumes made for easy gifts for the extended family who would soon descend upon the house like locusts.

"Is this all you have? Just clothes and shoes? I wanted the new iPhone," my sister asked.

I laughed. Even I didn't have one, it cost a thousand dollars!

After distributing the gifts, dinner was served. My father had slaughtered two of his chickens for me. My father's chickens ran around his yard, without any food ever provided save for water. They dug up worms and chased down termites. I had forgotten how fresh organically fed chicken tasted, bursting with concentrated flavor. In the US I told myself "food is food" because I couldn't afford to shop in the organic food section. The chickens I was used to buying in North Dakota were twice the size and tasted like their meat had been diluted with three parts water for every gram of meat.

My sister poured at least eight ounces of Fanta for each of the kids to have with their dinner.

"They won't drink anything but juice," she said.

I rolled my eyes, that was not juice.

"I have to go through ten liters a week because of that. They have juice in the morning instead of tea, juice at daycare, and juice at dinner," she said, proud of her children's uppity taste.

I had noticed the older one, Jayden, was a little plump. Again, I let it go.

My family wanted to stay up and chat about wildfires, earthquakes and mass shootings in North Dakota, things they figured affected my daily life, given the US news. I did not feel up to dissecting fact from fiction after such a long journey. I chuckled at how I would also have to do the same dissection in three weeks, dispel whatever stereotypes of Africa they too watched on TV, and explain that I wasn't visiting my family in some hut in a village with my pet monkey.

I excused myself and retired to bed, yet the room was so hot that I could not sleep. I missed the air conditioning and cool winter nights of the Dakotas. Curling up in a ball, I felt disappointed in myself. Had I become the proverbial African who goes away for a few years and comes back acting like they're too good for the place? Was there room to bring a different point of view to my family, to my country, or would doing so mean I was losing my way? Becoming less Zimbabwean?

Exhaling, I promised myself that I would not comment negatively on anything for the remainder of my stay. I would speak to everyone in Shona, prove that stupid lady at the airport wrong, dress modestly, and eat whatever I was offered. A mosquito hovered over my ears right as I was finally slipping off to sleep. I let out a loud and uncharacteristic cuss, before quickly chiding myself. *Makanaka, this is home,* I reminded myself.

The next morning, hot water was boiled and poured in a bucket for me to dilute with the appropriate measure of cold water to bathe. The taps in Harare no longer produced running water so my parents frequently had large containers of water collected from a nearby borehole, despite the fact we lived in one of Harare's most upscale suburbs. I saved the soapy water in the bucket to flush the toilet with later. Breakfast was ready when I joined the family. The kids were watching cartoons.

"This is how they know so much English," my brother-in-law boasted. "We let them watch all day."

Again, I kept my tongue.

The maid served mashed potatoes, mincemeat, and baked beans. I was a little confused but remembered that before I left, we used to have spaghetti and meatballs for breakfast at eight in the morning. The portion was much too large for me, having been accustomed to eating only an egg or two for breakfast, or a small cup of yogurt and granola, or perhaps avocado toast if I was particularly hungry.

"Is that all you're going to eat? Even Jayden eats more than that," my brother-in-law said.

I wanted to say, "Jayden's great-grandmother died of heart failure, both his grandparents who are eating equally unwarranted portions have high blood pressure and diabetes and don't exercise, your wife had gestational diabetes and my poor nephew is already well on his way to being overweight." Instead, I smiled and said, "I'll eat more later."

Soon, the first wave of the locusts descended upon the house.

"Why do you keep speaking in Shona? Speak in English so we can hear if you sound American yet," they chided.

I smiled yet persisted with my Shona. I gave gifts of American chocolate that I'd bought after Halloween clearance at Walmart, perfumes from Burlington Coat Factory, a few items I found on the clearance rack at Ross, and indoor slippers from Dollar Tree. Gleeful aunts, uncles, and cousins broke into songs of gratitude when they received something they loved. I felt guilty for adhering too closely to my budget when shopping. If a few dollars brought this much joy, surely I could've spared more.

After their visit, my mother and I drove them home, stopping at the roadside for some traditional fruit sold from the back of a pickup truck. Mazhanje were dark brown on the outside with thick slimy yellow insides. All you can eat, with a large sack on the side for everyone spitting out their seeds. Stuff yourself full, then pick a few to leave with, all at a flat rate. I moaned in satisfaction as the scrumptious slimy flesh filled my mouth, sucking on the seeds until they were fully naked, then savored the skin, thick, dark brown with a burst of flavor at every chew. *This* was how to vacation at home. Americans could never understand the bliss of wild fruit, harvested from untamed forests that are rife with monkeys. All enjoyed on a roadside, from the back of a pickup truck, conversing with strangers whom I felt should be family because they were Shona, *my* people. Nearby stood a bald dark-skinned man grilling fresh maize on the roadside. I ran over to him and asked for two freshly grilled cobs. I closed my eyes as my tongue was delighted by tastes that had become a distant memory. For the first time in years, I felt alive again.

My mother's car was running low on gas, so we stopped at a fuel queue in Mabelreign. We queued for two hours, chatting while moving a few inches forward every five minutes. I'd never had to queue to fill my car up in North Dakota. When we were five cars from the pump, the attendant told us that the fuel had run out and we needed to go elsewhere. Frustrated, we drove to Greencroft, passing multiple empty fuel stations along the way and joining the Zuva petrol station queue at five in the evening. For an hour, we inched closer to the green and white filling station. Right at six o'clock, the attendant came to tell us they were closing, so we would have to return the following day. My mother drove home in silence, dejected, while I lashed out about the gas station attendants, the gas company, the economy, the government. I began feeling queasy as we got closer to Greendale, so joined my mother's silence and listened to my stomach bubbling instead.

Later that night, after dinner, I had to rush to the bathroom and barely made it to the toilet seat. I had a running stomach. Of course, everyone in the US talked about not eating from the roadside when traveling to developing countries, but this was my country. I was *not* supposed to get sick when I grew up eating this *very* food. As time passed, my mother knocked on the door worried. I did not want to tell anyone that I had diarrhea. Instead, I clandestinely asked her for a bucket of water to flush. She brought me one, but I needed more water just five minutes later. I called out for my mother, but she sent my sister instead with another bucket. Damn it, one more person who might get suspicious. Keeping the secret was impossible. By the end of the night and countless buckets of water later, everyone knew. My body was letting me down. I felt like it was telling me that I did not belong in my own country.

By the second week my stomach settled, and I played tag and hide and seek with my nephews. I watched multiple sunsets with them seated on my lap—Zimbabwe's spectacular skies tinted in hues of pink, purple, and orange. The giant sinking sun always appeared much closer to earth than it did in North Dakota. It was as if nature was trying to make up for the derelict buildings, roads, and water systems. My sister made fun of me for attempting to capture the sunset with my phone camera.

"Have you never seen the sun? Does it not exist in North Dakota?" she teased.

I ate matemba—tiny dried kapenta fish with sadza—when everyone else wanted rice and chicken, scrumptious flavors I'd missed that transported me to a time when I felt fully Zimbabwean. I picked fresh mangoes, avocados, and guavas straight from the trees in my father's yard. The bumpy pothole-laden drives to Avondale shops became a delight. Foodlovers market had the best pepper steak pies and beef samosas. Pick and Pay had delectable fresh cream donuts, covered in chocolate. Creamy Inn did not disappoint with its vanilla cones, which tasted just as I remembered them from my childhood. I indulged all without a care about the calories they carried, thanks to my family.

I found art for my apartment walls back in North Dakota and met the artists who carved the granite rocks and made the paintings. My favorite sculpture was of the flame-lily, Zimbabwe's national flower. We spoke in Shona, and I laughed at various headlines displayed in newspapers with strangers at the market. On one of my drives home, I bought a large pizza for a few beggars who sat on the side of the road and we shared it as we conversed about how hard it had become to make a living in our country with the hyper-inflation, no jobs, and crumbling infrastructure. Zimbabwe was using both local currency and US dollars but the black market exchange rate was higher. For the first time, I changed US dollars on the black market at Strathaven shops and felt so gangster afterward. My mother made fun of me for feeling like I had done something so scandalous.

For my last week before returning to the US, I was determined to explore more of the scenic side of Zimbabwe with my family. We took a road trip to Nyanga and I pulled out a playlist of songs that were hits when I still lived here. My family sang along and we taught my niece and nephew songs from a time before they were born. My nephew sat comfortably on the middle compartment, his back to the windshield as he wiggled his body in dance. I giggled at his lack of coordination and marveled at my ease with him seated there compared to that first drive back from the airport.

We spent the first day of our trip at Leopard Rock and took turns feeding zebras and kudus. I laughed at my brother-in-law after one zebra looked like it was charging toward him for more food when he'd run out. I recorded a video of his frantic face as he rushed to jump over the fence and the family threatened to post it on Youtube. He would be the key to riches for the family, we joked. I laughed until my stomach hurt, a welcome hurt this time. We went on a walking safari later in the day, took selfies with ostriches and wildebeests, and left our legs painted in dust. I taught the kids all the animal names in Shona, bribing them with candy should they get the pronunciation just right.

Two days later we hiked Mutarazi Falls, the second highest in Africa, and I convinced everyone except my mother to try ziplining over the gorge with me.

"Iye nyakuzvifunga anga abatwa neyi? They're asking for death," she insisted.

We made fun of her for being chembere—too old and set in her ways—as the rest of us got strapped in and screamed and cried like we were dying as we zipped over the gorge then laughed about it for days on end.

Stuck in the car together for a week, we had heart-to-heart conversations about how each of us had changed over the years, about our hopes and dreams, our fears and anxieties. We comforted each other, held hands, and shared meals.

On the last day of the trip, I braided cornrows into my mother's gray and black hair, and when I was done with my immaculate lines, Jayden remarked, "Gogo, you look like a zebra!"

Back in Greendale, I lay almost naked in my childhood bedroom, covering myself with only a sheet. I hadn't felt this content on any day over the last five years in America. A mosquito sang above my head in the dark, and I let its singing be the soundtrack to my last night at home, covering my body with a sheet to keep it from biting me. Even though my country was falling apart, was returning to work abroad again worth missing the moments and experiences I'd just had? I cried myself to sleep.

The Collector of Degrees

Your father was accepted into a Ph.D. program in the US shortly after graduating from NUST University in Zimbabwe. That was his first mistake; he should never have applied. Initially, he moved to Missouri alone. Then, as though it wasn't enough for one person to suffer, he applied for your mother and your siblings to join him. How stupid! I guess he couldn't have known. You were all admitted as dependents under his student F-1 visa, and now you've all been tethered to his sad immigration student status that has lingered for almost fifteen years. But wait, now *you* are attending community college, which means you can apply for your *own* F1 visa. You are about to break off, study, work hard, realize the American dream. Freedom is here, despite still living under your parent's roof. You are giddy!

You select biology, hoping to work in the healthcare sector. You've always had a heart for helping those in need. To pay for college, you work as a nanny, watching kids before class and braiding hair after, with hardly any time to rest. You can't take classes part-time. F1 students need to be enrolled in class full-time to be eligible for a visa. It is hard to make friends because of your schedule. College kids want to eat out, go skating, go out for drinks. You realize that you need money to make friends in college, money you don't have. Two years of toil grind away, and the work/study cycle finally comes to completion, with sleep-laden eyes and fatigue your closest companions. You did it! You walk across the stage clad in esteemed robes, the claps and cheers of your parents and siblings.

After graduation, you apply for your OPT card. It authorizes all foreign students to work in the country legally for a year after graduation. You find employment at a restaurant, a real company with coworkers, and work in the kitchen, cleaning dishes. All year you save because the following year, you need to return to school to complete your four-year degree. You will be out of status after the year of authorized work unless you do. As you complete the year of OPT at the restaurant, you meet Wole at your neighbor's Nigerian wedding. With an attentive ear, he woos you. As he peels you open over the coming weeks, you are amazed at how well he understands your family's immigration situation. He moved to the US as a college student and was unable to secure an H1b visa upon graduation. He is out of status, undocumented. You bond over your hatred of the US immigration system, the lack of a path to citizenship. Wole is working as a mechanic and convinces you to move to North Dakota. There is a need for labor there, he assures. You apply for college there, and as OPT wraps up, you move in with him, ready to start your four-year degree.

Wole asks you to be a witness at his court wedding. He has found a white, blonde American to marry for his papers. It is just business; he won't even move in with her; he'll simply change his mailing address to hers. After three years, he will divorce her and marry you. You testify under oath to USCIS that you have witnessed their love blossom. With conviction, you describe their relationship as though it is the one you share with him. You sign the marriage certificate plus a testimony that will be presented as evidence for his case despite the termites crawling in your heart in warning because you want to pretend that you've found your soulmate. Because you've seen your parents live without papers for decades, you understand that this is a necessity. Your parents have never returned to Zimbabwe for weddings, funerals, or vacations because of their immigration status. The last time they were in Zimbabwe, it was still Rhodesia. They don't even hold Zimbabwean passports; the process to get new ones is too convoluted with the independence from Britain. Your parents aren't in the country illegally; your father is in status, on a student visa, taking classes at a community college. He first came to the US for a three-year Ph.D. program because he already had a master's and was granted credits for it. But no one would sponsor his H1B visa after that, so he went back to school and got a second Ph.D. to prevent him from falling out of status. This time he studied geology, yet he still could not find a sponsor. The only way for him to remain documented is to continue going back to school to maintain his student status. Now, almost eighteen years later, he has two Ph.D. 's and five associate degrees, not to mention the master's and bachelor's degrees he earned in Rhodesia. Your poor mother is tethered to his F1 visa as a spouse, meaning she doesn't have an immigration status independent from him. She has had no right to work or study in the US for eighteen years. All she is legally permitted to do is to be a wife. You're not sure which of your parents you pity more.

You complete your four-year degree while living with Wole and become eligible for another year of OPT, a much-needed reprieve from the cycle of working and raising money for tuition. What a privilege to simply be able to work. This time, you work in a hospital, in the lab. Things are coming together. You study for your GREs and plan to enroll for your master's after the OPT year is complete.

When it comes time for Wole to divorce, he pays the woman for her service. Half the money is from your hospital lab tech job.

Finally, you can marry the love of your life and thus get your papers since he is now a permanent resident. You come home one night, and he is gone. He didn't say goodbye. He simply packed all his things and withdrew the savings from your joint account. He leaves you with a lease but not even enough money to buy a can of soup. After three months, a friend sends you a link to his new Facebook profile. He has married a Nigerian woman in Texas. You realize that you were nothing but subsidized rent, sex, and a free witness for his fake marriage.

You decide to move back in with your parents in Missouri and reapply to the restaurant. You leave the job at the hospital, even though it pays more because you know they will fire you as soon as your OPT card expires in two months; their software has already begun sending you reminders to present your new card, but the restaurant isn't that sophisticated, they only check the validity of the card on E-Verify on the date of hire but don't keep track of expiration dates. You succeed in transferring your enrollment to a campus in Missouri. The end is near.

Good news: something called DACA has just passed! It means those who entered the US as undocumented kids will be able to get papers. Your family rejoices, but you soon realize that only your younger sister is eligible, the one who decided she was done stacking degrees while working fifty hours a week illegally and dropped out of school, relinquishing her legal status, because DACA is only for those who were brought into the country as kids *and* are out of status or undocumented. Even though all your siblings were brought into the country as children, only your lazy sister is out of status, leaving you and your brother consumed in envy and anguish. Hamusakamboona kudada kwasisi vacho. Kutsenga mvura chaiko – Boy does she rub it in. This program should have been open to all of you. Now she flaunts her work authorization card as you toil at the restaurant, getting ready for graduate school. If you had the work authorization she has, you could get another job in a hospital in Missouri and actually use your biology degree.

Your older brother gets married to a woman he met on Christianmingle.com. She's a single mother whom you promptly stereotype as desperate, damaged goods. Why else would she marry someone she's only ever met in person twice before? You judge her for being overweight and generally unkempt – Mungati kunyangara ikoko? Apa ndidhunda. Your brother is six foot three and a soccer player with an engineering degree. In the real world, he's a ten, and she's at best a four with baggage. The entire family smiles and wishes your brother well. You suspect he doesn't love her but is tired of stacking degrees, so you refrain from judgment, at least verbally. At their wedding reception, no one tells him that his bride is beautiful. You don't want to lie.

You smile at the cameras at your Master of Speech Pathology graduation, your third degree. This is the end of the road. You strike poses and take pictures while jumping and tossing your cap in the air, feet flying, and toes pointed at the sky. Look who's finally a professional! With your new OPT card, you leave the restaurant and land a job as a speech therapist. Your patients range from old men to little children and women your age. The love you have for them is something you didn't think you could feel for someone you weren't related to. This is the happiest you've ever been. The joy you experience when an R is pronounced for the first time when a few sentences are strung together without a stutter gives you a sense of fulfillment. Money is beginning to flow like never before— for a blissful six months.

Your employer gives you the news that they cannot sponsor your H1B, you only have a few months before OPT expires, and you will be fired. The automated emails reminding you to bring your new proof of employment start rolling in from HR *four* months before the expiration date. How do you explain that you can't?

You quit your dream job even though you have a month left on the card. You reapply to the restaurant once more. As long as you're legal on day one, you're safely back in the system, though your salary goes from thirty-five dollars an hour to eight dollars an hour, scrubbing plates.

You watch college classmates on Instagram as they globe-trot and pose before the Eiffel Tower, the Colosseum, the Egyptian pyramids, and even the Victoria Falls. Through your tears, you like and comment with a smiley face and heart emojis and type: *I'm so happy for you. Enjoy!* Secretly, you hope they catch malaria, Ebola, or some disease as exotic as all their destinations. You've never seen Victoria Falls, even though it is in the country of your birth, yet here are Americans riding elephants in your homeland. They get to be their fullest self in the US and go to your country and live their fullest life there, too. You wonder if you should consider it your country, you haven't been there since you were five years old, you don't speak the language, and have no memories of your time there.

Intermingled with the posts of those flaunting their travel are those happily in love. They post engagement rings, wedding ceremonies, baby bumps, and keys to their newly financed homes. You hope they're not truly happy, that their boyfriends are having affairs, that breakups are imminent. You hate that you've become this spiteful, but it's hard to be happy about their relationships when you realize that you need a sham marriage to stay in the country. Something like Wole's arrangement or your brother's, though you would never dare say that to his face. While you desire to fall in love, you've discovered men run away once they find out you don't have permanent papers. They think you're just a green card digger. You're not *just* that, though. Can't you find true love with someone who just happens to also be a citizen or permanent resident? You will truly love and serve your husband till death do you part. The papers are simply a package deal. Previously, you judged people who married to get their papers, but now you realize that you can't end up married to a *paperless* "love of your life" or you'll be in a situation like your parents, neither able to provide a path to citizenship for the other. You can't become your father, a forever student at his age.

To stay in status once more as the OPT card expires, you enroll in community college. You hate the struggle of asking family friends for their bank statements to prove that you have thirty thousand dollars available so you can be issued F1 status. You can present their statements, say they'll be your sponsor, but no one ever checks whether they ever contribute a dime or not; it's just a formality, one more piece of red tape to jump over. This time, you decide to study coding, the newest, most hip skill. Perhaps that might open some doors for you. They say Silicon Valley sponsors H1Bs and doesn't care if employees have degrees or not. To maintain your sanity, you take a fun class each semester. By graduation, you've taken painting, cooking, theater, and classical music, all while working forty hours a week at the restaurant. Every penny you've ever made goes to rent and tuition, and you have begun ducking family friends from whom you borrowed money with the promise of paying them back someday. You know now that that day will never come. You've never been eligible for student loans, and every friendship you've ever had has ended because you borrowed money to pay for school but were never able to repay it.

After graduating with your coding skills, your fourth degree, you aren't eligible for the year of OPT work authorization that students receive after completing a degree. You don't get the one-year reprieve of full-time work without full-time school because it's only granted provided the degree you just graduated with is a higher level than the last. Your last was a Masters, so... You knew that but needed to remain in status and couldn't afford to pay for a Ph.D., so community college once more it was.

You spend a month locked inside your apartment. Who could you possibly vent to? You can't talk to your parents because they've been in this situation longer and somehow have managed to convince themselves that this hell they created by immigrating was the best decision for the family, a cover for their guilt for this miserable life they handed their kids, you conclude. They remind you that life for immigrants was never meant to be lived like that of your American peers.

You contemplate moving back to Zimbabwe, but you don't know anyone there, and all you read in the papers are stories of hyperinflation, drought, unemployment, and people fleeing for South Africa. It sounds worse than the reality you're living in right now. At least here you know where your next meal will come from. You only have two months to re-enroll in college to keep your status, but you let that lapse because of your depression. You're told you need to apply for F1 reinstatement. You fell out of status *after* DACA was passed, so you're not eligible for that either. You can't afford an immigration lawyer, so you find websites that detail how to be reinstated, and you submit the required documents, praying you did it correctly. You've thought about simply being undocumented, but as a student, you know that at least ICE can't deport you, so you keep studying. USCIS sends you a letter telling you that they have a backlog for processing applications. The college allows you to enroll for your fifth degree anyway. Perhaps the reinstatement can be backdated.

Another graduation comes and goes. This time you took all the easiest classes, not caring about what was fun or useful. Silicon Valley never responded to any of your applications, not even so much as a screening interview. You stopped attending graduation ceremonies after the Masters. They are too depressing, a reminder that you've reached a new milestone of failure, another dead end. You learn the hard way that applying for F1 reinstatement is an ordeal, and should you let that happen once more, it would be a sure denial. There is no room to be depressed; you learned the hard way. If you can't even be a student to remain in the country, then what? You have two months to enroll in a sixth degree in case the reinstatement application is granted.

You bite your nails as you scroll through your phone in search of friends to borrow bank statements from for the new F1 admission. Instagram might provide some insight on who might have a little to spare. Everyone on your feed is someone you went to some college or another with. You hate those you graduated from the speech therapy program with who have been working for four years now. You do the math and realize that you have missed out on almost three hundred thousand dollars in wages while earning community college degrees you don't need. Community college is the cheapest, hence the most logical option. You give yourself a pep talk. You reassure yourself, telling yourself this can't go on for very long; eventually, things will work out.

Your phone rings. You drop it and cry; the screen cracks but continues blinking, a painful reminder that hazvina mupero – like your father, this could go on for decades longer, perhaps even unto your death.

Tsoro

Yes, get out of my way. Make room, part the red sea. Of course, all heads turn to behold me as I enter the sprawling Mediterranean-style mansion, mesmerized, so predictable. Keep that stride, long confident steps, perfectly sculptured brown legs peeking as my turquoise pleated midi-skirt sways, my red-bottom pumps echoing the confidence of my stride with a steady, consistent tap on the hardwood floor. Let the glow of the sun that peaks through the large arched glass windows turn my skin golden, let my black hair shimmer in the brilliance, and watch as my eyes turn into a fiery orange-brown in the sun's glow – Amai ndakanaka amai. Chin up and look straight ahead, girl; they might cower if your eyes meet theirs. Save the cowering for later. They've never beheld such beauty, such force, such elegance, such command.

I set my purse, bright orange and shearling, on the dining table. Conversation and chatter cease. I give them a second to catch their breath and scan the room quickly—typical white men of varying ages in boring black suits. I notice two women in the corner, flat shoes, heads slightly bent facing the floor, stealing glances as though they need permission to be in the room. I clear my voice, puff my chest up, and speak loud enough for everyone to hear. "Good afternoon!"

Silence. Sigh—they need more recovery time. But I press on. "I'm Chiedza, your new Director of Infrastructure and Development."

I watch them shift their hands, unsure of where to place them. In their trouser pockets, folded on their chests, scratching their heads. They exchange looks, turning their heads to face each other, forming soft frowns, squinting as though the sun's rays are blinding them. An older man with a face woven in wrinkles, a sagging, loose skin, double chin, and white hair paces back and forth. In a dark blue suit with pink checkered lines, the young man next to him is clearly a rebel, deviating from the plain black of the rest, grins excitedly. I spot Peter, the founder and CEO of Solartronics, who interviewed me. He is at least six foot five and has dark brown hair that he clearly dyes as his gray roots are peaking out. He steps forward and begins to clap. A crystal chandelier hangs above him. Behind him, the backyard is visible through the glass doors that lead to the patio. Beyond the fire pit, an Olympic-sized pool shimmers, surrounded by perfectly manicured Tuscan-looking bushes, and a large fire-pit with outdoor couches sits to the left.

"Welcome to Wisconsin, Chiedza!" he announces as he approaches me.

One person claps. Peter waves his hands, encouraging the others to join in the clapping. Slowly, lazy applause erupts across the room. Chatter resumes as Peter shakes my hand.

"She's the diversity hire," The older man with a sagging double chin whispers to those around him.

"I don't care. She's hot. Can I be her intern?" a young, blue-suited man responds eagerly.

I turn to face them sternly. Vati kudini? – Let the cowering begin. They fold their personalities into themselves, avoiding my eyes, crocheting their fingers, and turning their bodies away from me. The young man is still facing me; I try to meet his eyes but realize he's staring at my hips.

"Welcome to my house," Peter says as he motions for me to follow him. "I'm glad you could join the offsite. Let me introduce you to a few people." As we walk past the bar, I glance at the wine selection the server in a white shirt and black bowtie has on the table and pass. For a man with a house this big, Peter sure does have poor taste in wine.

We meander across the house, through carved wooden doors, rooms with exposed beam ceilings, as he introduces me to everyone. Every time he makes sure to mention, "She's from Zimbabwe. Isn't that cool!"

He never mentions my Ph.D. in Physics, the ten years I spent running the semiconductor fab at Intel, my research on the degradation of organic solar cells that was published in the *American Journal of Physics* and the *Nano Energy Journal*, or the deals I've brokered for John Deere and Tesla, despite everyone's clearly questioning *"why her"* faces. I'm pretty sure he heard that diversity hire comment as well. I laugh to myself. I guess I'll have to get Peter in line as well. This will be fun!

"Where did Peter say she's from?" one of the two women in the room whispers behind me.

"I don't know, but she's some type of foreigner," the other responds.

Peter introduces me to the circle of people that has the old man and young kid last. I wonder if he thinks I should've forgotten the whispered words by now. "This is Chuck, VP of Engineering," Peter says as he gestures towards the old man.

I cuss internally, realizing the old man he is going to be my boss, he reports to Peter. Chuck chews loudly on his shrimp cocktail and nods, looking straight ahead at the aquarium.

"And this little guy is Jake. He's like a son. His dad and I go way back. We went to Stanford together, and I'm so proud that Jake is following in our footsteps. He'll be interning with us for the summer. I told his dad that Jake will always have a job at Solartronics," Peter says proudly before saying Greek letters in random order. Jake repeats them, and they both beat their chests twice with closed fists.

"So, what's your background?" Jake asks. I'm pleasantly surprised. He's the first to ask. I happily recite my decorated resume, highlighting my awards and dropping names where I see fit. From the corner of my eye, I can see the expression on Chuck's face change. He is clearly impressed. The others cower once more. That's right, bow down—I know my stuff, and I'm going to shake things up over here. Before you know it, I'm going to run this place.

"That's so impressive. I'd love to learn more from you. I just finished my freshman year with a 4.0, but I don't have a clear direction on what I want to specialize in. Peter, may I work with Chiedza for the summer?"

"Of course!" Peter says without hesitation.

Great, I get to babysit a frat boy! I'm going to have to find a way to lose him, quickly. Overload him with work, give him impossible deadlines, make him read research papers that are far too advanced for him, send him off to towns in the middle of nowhere, Wisconsin, to scout out new solar business partnerships with farmers—he'll be whining to Peter about how awful I am in no time, asking for a transfer. I smile at Jake and shake his hand firmly, squeezing it tightly and holding the crushing clasp for a few seconds to assert myself. He winces and I let go – Usandijairire. Shaking his hand to get blood flow back, he takes a step back, sizes me from my shoes to my hair, then purses his lips as though he's about to whistle.

"Damn!" he says loudly. I smile.

"Lastly," Peter keeps going, "this is David. He's our Director of Quality. He's your counterpart, also reporting to Chuck."

In his mid to late thirties, David looks to be about my age, and he's good-looking. I notice a ring on his finger.

"David has been here almost fifteen years. Started as an intern when the company only had thirty people. He told me then he wanted to run this company someday, and I knew instantly he had the grit and would do whatever it takes to be at the helm someday."

I stare at David's bland, black suit. He fits right in with the rest of the old crew. I will have to keep a close eye on this guy, but if his strategy is simply to blend in and maintain the status quo, I have nothing to worry about. David nods his head at me. I do the same.

Peter walks to the center of the room and stands next to the double magnum bottle of champagne to begin a toast. "What a rollercoaster this has been! After a scary year, we can finally press forward with hope and a winning spirit."

The crowd cheers and raises their glasses. I look at David, who is fidgeting with his ring. He recognizes the confusion on my face and leans over to explain as Peter carries on.

"Peter didn't tell you? We were about to declare bankruptcy, but Jake's dad stepped in and gave Peter fifty million dollars to pay off debt and invest in new technology. Peter is going crazy trying to change the company's image and reinvent us with the latest equipment, and," he pauses and looks at me, "you know," he adds as he accepts a glass of wine from a server's tray.

"The little intern has been so annoying, walking around like it owns the place because of it's father's investment. Literally anything it suggests, Peter treats as gold. I guess he wants a good report back to Daddy after the summer. Good luck with that." David turns his head and joins the crowd in clapping and cheering at whatever Peter has just said as if he heard it.

I follow suit, but all I think about is the fact that I just sold my house in Miami and moved to Wausau, Wisconsin, and the president of the company I made these life changes for neglected to mention an impending bankruptcy. I exhale to calm myself, balling my hands into fists.

I try to focus on what Peter is saying. "To incentivize the employees, we are putting in place an aggressive tiered bonus structure. And at the end of the year, we will *all* vote for the employee who has contributed the most value to Solartronics—has led the pack in turning our business around. They will get a million dollars."

The crowd gasps. David drops his glass to the floor, spilling red wine on my shoes and sending tiny shards of glass across the floor. Peter laughs and raises his glass in our direction. "Yes," he continues, "whatever it takes, folks. Go big for Solartronics!"

The crowd continues to cheer. The servers ignore me as if they can't see the wine pooling at my feet. I make my way to the kitchen to find some paper towels. Alone amidst the stainless-steel appliances and an oversized island full of appetizers—bacon-wrapped shrimp, fried avocado, sliders, charcuterie boards with the widest cheese selection I've ever seen—I take a deep breath. A million dollars? A million dollars? Oh, you haven't seen the majesty of me. You have no idea what I'm capable of, what I can accomplish, the hardships I've had to bear, the depth of my resilience. That check is mine! I sit in silence for a few minutes, daydreaming about the possibilities.

"Oh, there you are!" Peter says, startling me from behind. I reach for the paper towel and wipe my shoes. "Are you ok? We got a server to clean up the glass," he says.

"Yeah, not to worry," I respond. David and Chuck follow Peter in the kitchen. I see the competitive yet desperate spirit rising within them. A childlike desire to be noticed, to be reassured, to become the favorite, engulfs their countenance. They follow him like puppies begging to be pet.

"Let me show you something," Peter says excitedly as he leads me to the fridge. A picture of a little black girl with a bald head and sad eyes rests on the counter, next to the fridge. "I sponsored a kid from Zimbabwe when I found out that's where you're from. The website had an interesting story about how tough her life is and what my money will do for her. Really reminds you about how lucky we have it out here," he says proudly.

I stare blankly at him. I've always been astonished by people who display their small acts of charity so publicly. Is she meant to be a conversation starter? Do the child's parents want her face displayed in a stranger's home? Do they want hers to be the official face of poverty? What will she grow up to be? Does she not get a chance to share her story however she chooses to? Do people really give so little that they feel the need to plaster it on display for the world to see when they do? If anyone in my family or I put up a picture of everyone we help on an ongoing basis, there would be no room in the house. I suppress the urge to laugh. Instead, noticing that her name, Fadzai, is the same as my little sister's, I feign a smile and teach Peter how to pronounce the "dz" sound correctly. "Just like you pronounce my name." Much to his delight.

"Doesn't she have the cutest accent?" he says to Chuck. "I could listen to her speak all day!" He asks about my upbringing in Zimbabwe, and David, Jake, and Chuck listen in. I'm selective about what I share, focusing only on the triumphs along my journey, much to their disappointment. *A million dollars*, I remind myself—*you can stroke a few egos along the way*. "Well, Peter, this is great work you're doing," I say to shift the attention from my upbringing. "I bet you're changing this little girl's world."

Peter brightens. "Do you think we could do more philanthropy over there? It could all be part of our rebranding? I want to make a difference in the world, find purpose, you know?"

I laugh to myself. I know plenty of people who could use help; I don't need a website. "Tell you what, why don't I lead this venture for you, for the company? Maybe we could plan a few trips out there, couple them with some safaris or something," I say, though, in my mind, I'm thinking, just give me the money to support my family and friends in Zimbabwe. We can send you a picture if that makes you feel better about yourself.

Peter places his hands on his heart, his mouth hanging open in excitement; speechless.

"Let's not plan trips to Africa just yet," Chuck interjects, tapping his foot. "There's work to be done and plenty of places in the US where we can go for team bonding escapades."

"Yeah, Peter, why don't we plan something in Aspen or something?" David offers. "Peter, we all know you love to ski. Three days on the slopes sounds amazing, doesn't it? Jake, didn't your dad offer his place out there if we meet our year-end numbers?"

Jake's eyes caress my body. "There's a hot tub out there. It's always great to wind down there after a day on the slopes."

"I love it! Let's do it!" Peter says. "I'll tell Hillary to clear all your calendars over Christmas," he continues as he scurries out of the kitchen in search of his admin.

My trip to Zimbabwe is already booked. Because I don't make it home often, my family tends to take time off work to be with me. And now I have to cancel? Peter didn't even ask if the timing works for me.

"I hope you ski," David says spitefully to me before he follows Peter.

Before I have a chance to recover, Chuck walks over to me.

"Listen," he says. "I'm a very simple man to work for. You'll either love me or hate me. There's no in-between. You do what I tell you, and we'll be just fine. Get with David and he'll tell you my expectations for checking in with me. A morning report of how you plan to spend your day, a mid-afternoon check-in so I can redirect, if need be, and an end-of-day summary. Don't ever suggest anything to Peter directly without passing it through me. So that little performance you just gave, not ok," he says with a raised voice, his face directly in front of mine, so close I can smell his shrimp breath.

His wide shoulders hover over me. I freeze.

I'm a director! I will not be micromanaged like an intern. I will not allow my communication of ideas to the executive suite or board members to be edited, filtered, and possibly reclaimed with new ownership.

"Well, Chuck. I think we need to..." I begin but notice him lift his wrist and pretend to stare at his watch, intentionally communicating that he doesn't have time for whatever I have to say. I stop in disbelief.

"The baseball game is starting. Time to let loose. Business is done for the day. Pick your team carefully. This is Brewers' land," he says as he storms off. "Oh," he stops, turns back to me, and adds, "and I play a round of golf on Fridays, so don't disturb me tomorrow."

I hope he gets hit with a golf ball this weekend and never returns.

"He's right, you know," Jake says, startling me. "Lots of Brewers fans out here." I'd forgotten he was still in the room. "We start every Monday morning company meeting by discussing the game. They hate that I love the Giants, but I don't let them tell me what to do."

I don't know the first thing about baseball, but I'll learn so I can contribute to the conversation.

"Listen, do you want to grab dinner tomorrow?" he asks, leaning into me. "I can give you some insights about the company."

I want to squash this kid! I'm at least fifteen years older than he is. He's clearly the kind of kid who has always gotten whatever he wants. It's clear the fascination here, the one toy he's never had access to is a Zimbabwean one. I know I'm a creature that intrigues. Many a man have fallen in a single evening. But he doesn't know who he's dealing with. I will have him wrapped around my little finger. Some toys are dangerous, kid. You might lose a finger... or two.

"Let's join the group for the game," I say as I follow the cheers in the living room. I sit quietly, alone, in the back, watching my new coworkers react to balls being tossed, flung in the air, and uniformed men running around a field. Ndoitamba sei Tsoro iyi? – There are a million dollars at stake. How do I solve this puzzle, ensure the money is mine?

When I was a little girl growing up in Mutare, Zimbabwe, we used to play a two-person mathematical strategy game called Tsoro. Each player dug ten holes in the ground and filled each hole with two seeds. The starting player selected which of their holes they wanted to play from first and dictated the direction the game would go, clockwise or anticlockwise, and that direction would have to be followed for the rest of the game. They move the seeds forward according to the rules and either gain more seeds or lose a turn. The game ended when one player had captured all the seeds in the holes. The winner kept all the seeds. I'd have to play my own game of Tsoro with each coworker. They'd all gotten a first-move advantage.

First, Chuck must go. I need to get him fired as soon as possible. I can't work for a prick. Jake is an easy pawn, and he's already taken a liking to me. I can use him to get Peter's ear. Make him sing my praises but loathe Chuck. If Jake says enough about Chuck's incompetency, he'll be gone. Better yet, what if Jake's dad said Chuck must go? David, I can keep, make it seem like I have competition. Besides, he doesn't seem to have a solid strategy. Peter's ego is so small, I can stroke it all over the place; it won't take long for him to favor me over David.

I took this job because I did research on how we could use existing dying Solartronic film technology to create new organic solar cells with increased efficiency, plus reduced or minimized degradation. I believe we can create a new type of cell that could have a far-reaching impact in providing supplemental energy and helping the planet go green. Farms could power bigger and heavier equipment and function fully off the grid. We could even incorporate these cells into clothes and use them to charge phones while running or to power tents for campers. Most of all, the cells would be cheaper than any existing material. If this works, Solartronic could become a billion-dollar company in a few years. I look over at Chuck and click my tongue in annoyance. But what do I know? I'm just the diversity hire.

"Chiedza, will you bake the cookies for Monday's celebration?" Peter says, interrupting my thoughts.

"You got it, Peter!" I respond.

I have no idea what they are celebrating. I also don't know the first thing about baking cookies. The room erupts in cheers as the ball flies across the field on an eighty-inch TV. I pull my phone out and google Jake's father. If he's driving funding for this company, I need to find out more about him. What's he into? What's his background? How can I leverage his connections and existing businesses to add value for him? What will it take to impress him? I'm delighted to find a plethora of information about him online. I could read up on him for days. I lean over and whisper in Jake's ear. "Just between you and I, can I meet your dad? I might be willing to grab that dinner tonight."

His eyes light up. "Yeah!" he responds enthusiastically.

I smile. Let the games begin.

Unseen

"**P**unch my eye as hard as you can!" Tatenda shouted as she attempted to break up her brother's wrestling game and have one of them fight her instead. The boy's tattered clothing was covered in gray dust, which looked like ash against their black skin. The boys ignored Tatenda, pinning each other on the littered sidewalk as cars sped past them, honking for them to get further out of the way. She searched the distance for Baba's return from work; perhaps she could get to him first, then it might not matter that the boys didn't want her. Women wearing brightly colored *zambiyas* around their waists, with babies on their backs and buckets filled with different kinds of fruit, scolded the boys to get out of the way as they walked by in brisk steps. The smell of roasting maize cobs filled the air, making her hungry. The man roasting the cobs on an open fire by the street corner called out enticing deals to those passing by. Tatenda shouted from the bottom of her lungs to get her brothers' attention once more, though she knew today wouldn't be any different; they would never let her play.

Farai pinned Joshua's head to the ground, right next to the curled banana peel on the roadside. He sat on Joshua's torso and sang, "I win! I win! Race you back home!" before jumping up and dashing into the sunset. Joshua got up, determined not to lose the race as well, and sped behind him.

"Wait for me! I can run fast too!" Tatenda said to the wind as she followed as quickly as she could, but they faded into the distance.

By the time she arrived home, both Joshua and Farai were in the outpost bathroom arguing about which of them was stronger. Tatenda stood outside and interjected, "If you let me, I can beat up both of you." The boys carried on as though she wasn't present. The street dog barked aggressively at her father as he entered their yard. Its ribs were exposed through its fur. It was a wonder the dog was still confident enough to instigate brawls with passersby. She ran up to her father and asked how his day was.

"Where are your brothers? I have something for the men of the house," he said as he took his shoes off to enter the home. Tatenda stared at the shoes in envy. He was still able to bend his big toe so it wouldn't protrude onto the road as he walked, unlike hers. The soles around his heels were almost gone, despite the front of the shoes being as good as new, a reflection of his confident walk that made him appear as though his toes floated in the air, too good to touch the streets of Kambuzuma. As he sat on the sole wooden chair in the room, her mother knelt before him and clapped in welcome, head bowed.

"Tatenda, follow me. Let's serve dinner," Amai motioned to her. She got up and followed her mother.

Seated before Baba, the boys, who'd dusted themselves but neglected to change, greeted him. Baba smiled, exposing his teeth, and reached for his bag.

"These are for you." He held out two math books, one for each of the boys. "Education is how men provide for their families. You better listen in school and study these for practice."

"*Maita Baba*," her brothers chanted as Tatenda placed plates full of *sadza* and collard greens before each of them. They eagerly dived into their food, flipping through their books with fingers filled with sticky sadza and vegetables.

"Where is mine? Tatenda sulked. "I'm learning to read at school, too."

Baba ignored her and turned instead to Amai. "I brought some beef for us to enjoy tomorrow," he said. The family cheered, having not had a taste since last Christmas.

Baba's Motorola phone beeped, and he flipped it open. Silently, he read and chuckled, then passed it to her brothers, who, in turn, laughed. She leaned over to peek, but her oldest brother shoved her away.

"It's not for girls!" he said as he handed the phone back to their father. Baba smiled and returned the phone to his pocket. He reached for a plastic bag and took out two books, one for each of her brothers.

"You boys are going to be businessmen someday. Keep studying," he said as he distributed equal pats on the boy's backs. Tatenda turned to her mother in protest.

"It's ok, you learn to cook, you clean, be a good woman, and someday, you too will find an educated man to marry," her mother said to console her. Amai worked as a maid for a wealthy family in the Northern Suburbs, preparing all their meals each day to supplement the family's income. "I can begin to teach you tomorrow since it's Saturday. No more playing in the streets with boys as though you're one of them." Tatenda feigned a smile.

Amai woke her up as the sun's rays began to peer to the yard. "You must learn how to behave, and this begins with waking up on time." Tatenda dressed with sleep-filled eyes, donning a yellow dress that had clearly seen too many washes. She learned how to clean, how to pour Jik into the toilet and scrub until she almost suffocated from the rising bleach fumes. Tatenda made lunch with

Amai, learning how to dice tomatoes and onions into perfect cubes. She made the Covo vegetables in the afternoon and, because she had done so well, she would cook the special meat for dinner, under Amai's supervision, of course. Amai carefully explained the instructions, taking time to show her when to add another log to the fire, when to add the oil, how often to turn it with the wooden spoon, the right amount of salt and Usavi mix, and the right temperature to allow it to simmer. Tatenda nodded her head in excitement, probing for clarification when Amai went too fast. A blue Honda Fit honked at the gate; it was Amai's boss. There had been a family emergency, and they needed Amai to watch the kids overnight while they went to Gweru.

Beef was always to be boiled to soften it before sautéing. The neighborhood could tell something special was being cooked. Even before she began frying, the smell of boiling meat wafted through the neighborhood, summoning those hoping to be invited to feast. Once Tatenda decided the meat was done, she poured oil into a pan and placed it on the open flame, grateful for being trusted with such an important responsibility. "Mucharuma zvigumwe," she said to herself with a smile – This would be the best stew anyone had ever had. They'll talk about it all night. Meticulously, she drained the boiled meat from the larger pot and dropped it into the searing oil, careful to save the beef broth for soup. As the meat hit the pan, a few droplets of oil splashed onto her cheeks. Tatenda groaned and ran to wash her face, wondering if they would leave a trace. It might be great for her neighbors and classmates to ask what happened to her face; she consoled herself. That way, she could tell them she was cooking meat. They would know her family was wealthy enough to enjoy some when it wasn't even Christmas.

The nosy woman next door, Mai Banda, whom Tatenda was certain was a witch, called her mother's name. The smell of searing meat was now undeniable, and the subtle peeks would soon turn into visitors with questions, a front for seeking an invitation. She had to keep the scavengers away. Tatenda ran over to distract the witch. She mentioned no one was home, but Mai Banda kept asking questions while peeking over to the fire. Unable to get a clear answer on when Amai would return from Tatenda, she clicked her tongue and muttered undeterred, "I'll be back."

Feeling proud of herself for getting rid of Mai Banda, Tatenda turned to walk back to her pan, just as a larger fire engulfed it and thick dark gray smoke arose. She screamed, her heart racing. Attempting to remove the pot from the fire, Tatenda seared her hand and knocked the pan over. Charred chunks of meat fell to the ground. She grabbed a bucket of water and tossed it over the fire, just in time for Mai Banda to peek over the fence and laugh.

Farai and Joshua got home first. "Is that the meat? Wait till Baba arrives! Ucharohwa!" they jeered to scare her.

Tatenda ran into the house, fighting back the tears, but they followed her. It was a strange feeling. She had spent her life trying to get their attention, yet they never as much as acknowledged her presence. Now they wouldn't let her have a mere second to herself. Why didn't they pay this much attention to her when she wanted to talk or play with them? If only this was the norm. She bit her lower lip, folded her arms, and soaked in the attention with trembling hands.

She heard Baba's roar from a distance, though she couldn't make out his words. Something about his money, stupidity, carelessness, disappointment, and punishment. Her teeth chattered as his footsteps grew closer. Tatenda curled into a ball until she felt his presence tower over her. She braced herself for a strike. From the corner of her eye, she fixed her attention on the grass-threaded broom in the corner and Joshua's old blue t-shirt, which doubled as a mop during the rainy season.

"Get up!" he yelled. "Where is your mother? How could she be so irresponsible, leaving you to finish the cooking alone?" Tatenda swallowed hard and kept her eyes focused on his shoes. Baba pulled her to her feet and with bulging red eyes and looked into her eyes.

He didn't lay a hand on her like her brothers had surmised he would. Instead, he spoke directly to her—albeit in anger—but he spoke to *her* all the same. Before now, he had spoken only to Amai, Joshua, and Farai. Despite his clenched fists, she could not help but feel warm, strangely comforted. She took in how his left eye twitched, how his neck muscles protruded, how he exposed both his top and bottom teeth when he spoke, how it was as though there was no one else in the room but her. This is not how she had hoped to get him all to herself, but she had finally figured out how to matter.

Over the coming weeks, she tried to replicate ways to get this unwavering attention once more. She stole mealies from the man at the corner street, tore her brothers' beloved brand-new textbooks, exchanged her dresses for fruit from women in the street, and wore her brothers' clothing instead. Each time she received varying levels of chiding from both her brothers and father, leaving her feeling accomplished. She competed with her brothers over grades, stealing their books then burning them when she was done with them, declaring she was smarter and she would be the new man of the house. "I'll go to America and be successful someday. Be richer than both Farai and Joshua," she sneered. Her brothers wrestled her, Baba spent evenings scolding her, Amai cried herself to sleep, and so she learned, if she wanted to be special, be seen, she had to be different, break every expectation.

After six years of basking in constant bickering with Baba, she completed high school with straight A's. Amai was sure to spare her some money to go to the internet café behind Baba's back as she secretly applied for scholarships.

• • •

AN ACCEPTANCE LETTER CAME in a large white envelope stuffed with magazines. She had to pick it up from her high school because they couldn't receive mail at home. Their home was in an illegal settlement. Tatenda was on her way to freedom, to America. Mai Banda stopped by, as did the rest of the neighborhood with their advice. Her father had two orders: "Don't lose your roots playing with white colonialists. And may I never hear that you have an American boyfriend."

• • •

BALTIMORE WAS A DISAPPOINTMENT. She felt like *it* was rebelling against *her*. Going against every expectation of America she had. The US was supposed to be glamorous, but zvipiko? Occasionally, she spotted a rat. They were not supposed to exist here! Morgan State University was eighty percent black. How was she to rebel and send her parents photos with white friends so they could worry that she was losing her roots? The food had no taste, and the campus didn't have flashing lights, like pictures of Times Square. In the few ways in which Baltimore behaved as expected, covered in lawn and concrete, it depressed her. She felt sorry for the soil underneath, kept captive, grains of dust not allowed to rise and cuddle humans.

What she despised the most was that no one on campus noticed her. No matter how hard she tried. There were other women with shaved heads, and all the women wore men's clothes, jeans, and pants. You hardly found a female in a dress. For everything that invited horrified looks from her father, for everything once forbidden or frowned upon, she found an entire club dedicated to it here. Tatenda didn't know how to be disobedient anymore, how to draw disgusted looks by stating her interests or ambitions. No longer was she first in her class. Both girls and boys had better grades than her. She found herself in the middle of the curve. Although she was failing one of her classes, she told her family that she was top of her class and everyone in Baltimore already knew of her genius. None of the girls could cook; most kept their rooms a mess, their beds unmade each morning. She stopped shaving her head once she arrived in America and realized, no one on campus cared or noticed her for it. Strangely, this was alienating; finding so many like-minded people should've given her solace, but now she simply blended in.

Worst of all, she realized she never really liked all those things she did in Kambuzuma. She just embraced them as her personality to make her brothers and father speak to her.

Sitting in her bed in the dorms that evening, Tatenda looked out her window at the sea of educated women. Baba was right about her struggling once she arrived. She was working in the campus kitchen, cleaning dishes, though she told her family she had an office job and even sent them pictures of her posing in the library—her "office." Tatenda took pictures in her friend's silver Lexus while seated in the driver's seat and told them that she had already saved enough to buy a car because America was the land of plenty. Baba seemed immune to her so-called success. So, she decided to tell him all about her American boyfriend. His anger pulsated through the phone, much to her delight. "I'll send you a picture next time," she said. As they argued, she felt her low-grade depression fade, satisfied that she had crested his anger, even though there was no boyfriend.

Although she had figured out how to keep her father engaged, riled, she couldn't seem to find a way to get a reaction from anyone on campus. She missed the ubiquity of what was considered acceptable in Kambuzuma. People generally agreed on what was culturally acceptable and what wasn't. It made figuring out how to be noticed uncomplicated. Here, she could declare that she wanted to be an astronaut or had given up on school and would drop out and still not get a reaction quite like the one her father would give her. It was overwhelming; she suffocated in the sea of freedom.

• • •

HE FIRST SAT NEXT to her in a statistics class. She took notes frantically whilst he scrolled through his phone. Tatenda was sure he would fail, but when their first test grades were revealed, he had received a B and she a D. Determined to find out how he had managed that, she began to chat him up, asking how he spent his time outside of class. She learned his name was Bao; he was a Chinese American.

His parents had moved to the US as college students and stayed after graduation. Bao and his sister were born in the US, though they spoke fluent Mandarin. His voice was a firm baritone, and he had gentle, kind eyes. He asked thoughtful questions of her, and school seemed to come to him without the striving she was accustomed to. Sure, she had been the smartest kid in her high school, but she had also done nothing but study. Tatenda loved how Bao stuck out on a campus with hardly any Asians. She noticed the glances they received whenever they walked together, the secret whispers. Others thought they were a couple, didn't they? And what a rare combination. With that, Tatenda asked him if he would be her boyfriend.

• • •

AN UNARMED BLACK MAN was shot by police, and images of the encounter were plastered all over social media. The conversation around police brutality dominated the news. Marches and protests were held on campuses around the nation. Tatenda had been cloistered on the campus since she arrived two years ago; she didn't drive and rarely ventured off the premises. Keenly, she listened to the storyline, picking up fragments of American history. There was collective anger, especially among black students. She was sad for the man who died and gathered that she ought to be angry like other students, but she didn't quite feel the emotions as deeply as they did. They shared stories about racism in America, about how black people had been disadvantaged since slavery, since the Jim Crow Era. Everyone on campus was much richer than her neighbors in Kambuzuma, so she didn't understand what they meant by income disparity.

Although she was studying on a full scholarship, she believed she had come this far on her own as a foreigner in the land of plenty. She believed she stood on none of the shoulders of her ancestors. "I have cousins living in huts in a village in Zimbabwe, but I've risen while they've done nothing with their lives. I have worked hard, and now I have a job and extra income in America. What do you mean African Americans are disadvantaged because of their great-grandparents? You don't need a government handout if you work hard," she said to her black classmates. Collective fury arose, voices rumbling as a circle formed around her. Tatenda watched in fascination, her lips tingling. This was what she had been yearning for. They noticed her. Shaun recognized that she was an immigrant; she didn't have the full context, so he stepped in to explain to her that the opportunity for blacks to do well in the US was only available because of MLK and the civil rights movement. The class clapped in unison. Shaun soliloquized about growing up in the projects, something she had no awareness of. That night, Tatenda went to bed feeling whole for the first time in two years. Her classmates' fury had revitalized her; her energy had returned. She felt seen once more.

No one had explained to Tatenda that had her great grandmother not escaped the war in her Rhodesian village, Tatenda's trajectory would've been vastly different. Her great grandmother had trekked by foot to Mutare, the nearest city, a three-day journey, her toddler in hand, to live as a beggar on the street. Anything was better than being recruited for war and walking past dead bodies daily while fetching water from the river, living in constant fear for her life and that of her child. Tatenda's grandmother, having street smarts, took a bus from Mutare to Harare as a teenager, determined to make a better life for herself. There, she met and married a man who worked as a gardener for a white Rhodesian family. Together they built a house in the illegal Kambuzuma settlement.

Their daughter, Tatenda's mother, was often invited as a young girl to play with the Madam's children. There, she learned to read and speak English. She learned to cook the food they ate, strange meat like bacon and cereal doused in hot milk. It was these childhood experiences, paired with her ability to speak English fluently, that got her hired as a maid for the councilman.

Of course, when her grandparents passed, they left the Kambuzuma home where Tatenda had grown up to her mother. And had her mother not provided her with money to go to the internet café,

Tatenda wouldn't have been able to apply for a scholarship. Tatenda had succeeded against insurmountable odds, but to claim that she was in America because of her own might alone, that she wasn't standing on the shoulders of her ancestors, was a fallacy.

Tatenda, enthralled by her ability to elicit a passionate response from her peers, one that rivaled even what she was capable of drawing from her father or brothers at her best, began her research. All night she kept the lamp beside her bed on and googled the differences between conservatives and liberals. She discovered that ninety-five percent of black voters voted for Barack Obama. She read conservative blog posts and memorized their most polarizing arguments. It was the perfect setup. She couldn't be accused of being racist since she herself was black. She could ascertain that her experiences in America didn't match with the narrative that African Americans subscribed to, therefore, racism, income disparity, lack of equal opportunity, and police brutality were a fallacy.

That evening, she called her parents. She had sent them pictures of her Chinese American boyfriend. Her father threatened to disown her if she ever brought home such a man. "I can love whoever I want!" she yelled on the speakerphone. Her brothers grabbed the phone, begging her to break up with him. In the background, she could hear her mother's cries. Tatenda knew she didn't love Bao but enjoyed the attention she received not only from her family but also when they walked hand in hand around the city. The intrigued faces of strangers displayed their secret whispers. She hated that Bao never argued with her. He asked questions calmly whenever she tried to start a fight; he listened attentively. She didn't know what to do with that. Whenever she was mad about something he did or didn't do, he apologized. No one had ever apologized to her before. She decided he was dull, but he served a purpose.

She sat on Bao's lap, watching the evening news. Donald Trump was on the screen, refusing to acknowledge the concerns of the black community. Bao struggled to understand why she was so unsympathetic. It's not that she was heartless; she couldn't even bring herself to watch the videos of the murder. She simply didn't have a lifetime of experience navigating race in America. She didn't have stories from her grandmother about what growing up in the south was like. The confederate flags everyone demanded be brought down meant nothing to her. She had no idea who the men memorialized in the statues being torn down were or what crimes they had committed. Tatenda didn't drive and had not experienced the fear of being stopped by police. Besides, she had spent her life trying to appear strong, empowered, and in control. Something about admitting black people in living America were disadvantaged felt like an admission that she herself was hapless, to be pitied, a victim, and in need of rescuing.

President Trump's comments about immigration worried her. She knew she couldn't return to Zimbabwe the day she graduated. There were no employment opportunities in Zimbabwe; her fate would become just like that of any woman who had never been educated, never left Kambuzuma. To stay in the US required that she at least attempt to apply for an H1B, earn some money, and if she were to return, do so with enough money to buy her own home in the envied Northern suburbs. That would prove to everyone that she had, in fact, amounted to something. At this rate, by the time President Trump was out of power, if he stayed for eight years, there would be no path to citizenship for her.

At times, she had nightmares about getting off the plane in Harare with nothing in hand but her student ID. In the dream, all her relatives and Mai Banda gather around her, laugh, and point. They ask what else was to be expected to come from a girl child. Wouldn't the money have been better spent on either of her brothers? A democratic president would better her chances of pursuing her dreams in the US, of making something of herself before being forced to return right after graduation, but then again, if she voiced support for the democrats on this campus, she would find herself with the majority. How else could she be distinct, rare, worthy if she was ordinary?

Concerns about his stance on immigration, aside from Trump's comments about women, were at times reminiscent of what she spent her childhood rebelling against—misogynistic notions about women. She knew the burden that such notions could bring should they be permitted to flourish in the minds of society. Had this been the Zimbabwean president, she knew he would have her father's support. Had this been Zimbabwe, she would have been joining the protests and marches against his administration. However, as a black woman living in America, no one expected her to be an avid Trump supporter. She binged on FOX news to arm herself with all the arguments that his strongest supporters uttered, ready for a fresh opportunity to rile the crowds.

• • •

SHE OPENED THE BROWN package on her doorstep and eagerly unwrapped it. A bright red MAGA cap that she fit on her head now full of hair. Tatenda had also begun wearing dresses to class after noticing that people asked her why she was dressed up anytime she wore one. Ironically, she was forced to wear a dress every day as a young girl. Her mother and all her neighbors wore nothing but dresses, and she had rebelled by stealing her brothers' pants. Here, it was the dresses that distinguished her from the shorts, jeans, and yoga pants that dominated campus. Anytime she sent pictures back home, though, she was sure to be in jeans. Tatenda danced in anticipation of displaying her hat the next day.

Yellow leaves lightly fell to the ground, creating a soft carpet. The cold air was crisp and carried the scent of spicy pumpkin. Perhaps this was the one-way Baltimore didn't rebel: fall. A student jeered as she walked expectantly to class, clinging to her winter coat. She smiled in satisfaction and adjusted her hat. An orange cat walked in front of her, its tail dragging in the leaves. A man shouted that the president's rhetoric supported white supremacy. Tatenda stopped to engage him, reciting all the arguments she had heard on conservative media. She watched as emotion rose within the man and those around him, much the same way it used to rise in her father when she burnt the meat or shaved her head or told him she was going to be a more successful businesswoman than her brothers. Having had plenty of practice defending herself since the days of wrestling and playing Chihwande, she wasn't intimidated.

"How do you explain Africans doing well in this country while African Americans complain about white privilege? It has nothing to do with race. You all just have to work harder, pull yourself up by the bootstraps, and stop expecting handouts. Slavery was four hundred years ago," she said with a sly smile.

A large black woman in a bright red coat lunged at her, grabbed her hat, and threw it to the ground. "Aren't you worried about your immigration status after graduation?" she asked, remarking at her accent. "Illegals should be removed, and I too will happily and readily move back in with my loving family if things don't work out here after graduation," Tatenda replied calmly.

As she returned to her dorm that evening, she removed her hat, kissed it, and took a deep breath. She finally felt alive again. She would wear it again the next day, off-campus. Tatenda sat on her bed and powered on YouTube to watch a few more Trump videos. The first was of a convention filled with Trump supporters chanting "Make America Great Again." A sea of mostly white faces filled the stadium. The camera zoomed in on a few black supporters. She felt nauseous. She knew that had her college been in Mississippi, where confederate flags were celebrated, where crowds eagerly chanted MAGA, she would be exchanging her red hat for a Black Lives Matter t-shirt to evoke the emotions she was getting from her peers now.

Bao stopped in later that evening. He had heard about her escapade. Never had he been quite this worked up. It was exciting to see this side of him.

"I'm not going to support the democrats just because I'm black.

I'm allowed to have my own opinion. Isn't that what America is all about?" she protested calmly.

"This has nothing to do with your beliefs. You're looking for attention," he said in an accusatory tone that made her feel warm. Was that a spark of anger she was detecting?

"It's not my fault that people disagree with me. I am not going to be silenced," she said, raising her voice slightly and taking a step closer to him, hands on her waist.

Bao took a step toward her. She felt him about to explode and braced for herself for the ensuing passion, the fire she knew from her childhood. But instead of raising his voice, he lowered it. He put his hands on either side of her shoulders and looked her in the eye. "You are so beautiful, Tatenda, and smart and strong. You don't need to anger people. If I really thought you loved Trump's policies, I'd try to be supportive," he paused and cleared his throat. When he began speaking again, his voice had lost its foundation; it flailed with every word. His eyes turned glossy.

"In advancing your own agenda, you're invalidating the voices of black people who have grown up here. Those who understand the dynamics and lived experience of black America much better than you ever will," he said as he snorted mucus back up his nose.

"So now I can't speak because I'm not American? I thought liberals were all about immigrants. Or do you only want them when they agree with you? I'm still black and can write a book about how all of this racism stuff is nonsense if I so please," she said, heaving.

"You need therapy! I hope to God you stop striving so hard to be oppositional. I hope you try to understand the damage you cause. I can't be with you anymore, and this is not about Trump. It's just about your sick cries for attention," Bao said as they walked out of the room.

Tatenda stared at the blank phone screen, and tears streamed down, rebelling against her body's attempt to hold them captive. For the first time, she realized that she might have loved Bao. He was never dull; she just didn't know how to get a man to pay attention to her without picking a fight. She knew he was right, something was amiss with her, but she didn't know how else to be.

The room was silent. She listened for footsteps in the hall but heard none. Standing by her window, she watched light flakes of snowfall. Groups of friends laughed and chatted on the streets below. The pain of being alone sunk into her veins, so she decided to call her father.

"Baba, Bao and I are stronger than ever, and I am bringing home to pay *roora* in December." Her father responded that he would never accept that. He sounded weary yet inflamed.

"Ukamuunza pano, usadzoke kumba! You can no longer be my daughter," he asserted, his voice as firm and loud as the day she burnt the meat.

"Ndezvenyu izvo," Tatenda dismissed as though she didn't care. She imagined the twitch in his left eye, his protruding neck muscles, and took a deep breath before hanging up.

Consoled by the familiarity of his anger, she grabbed her Lenovo with renewed vigor and began a new google search: "How to plan a trip to the White House."

As the page struggled to load, the blue line at the top lazily crawling its way to the right, Tatenda felt a deluge of pain up within her. She embraced it, allowing it to take her captive, the tears to flow. With each buffering bar that loaded across the page, she daydreamed about an alternate life.

Ghost Of My Mother

My baby looked Zimbabwean on the outside, just like my mother, but on the inside, she was a foreigner. Don't be fooled by her large brown eyes, her full lips, or her unruly curls. Rangarirai couldn't utter a word of Shona; she despised our food and bore no knowledge of our customs or way of life. Who could blame her? I'd created this monster. I'd never had the time to teach her any of it, yet I despised her for behaving like an American. I often reminded her she wasn't one of them, but what did she know of Zimbabwe? She'd never even been there to visit. Besides, she didn't want to be associated with those primitive people in Africa, she'd say. The only Shona phrase she understood was Ndinokurova, meaning "I'll beat you," used not so much as an actionable threat but as a warning to behave.

I became pregnant by my African American college sweetheart after my first year in the US. He moved to Atlanta not too long after, leaving me to bear responsibility for the squiggly little life. She arrived with a scene, at her own timing, three weeks early and after seventy hours of labor. This was the first of many pains she would inflict on me.

As a single mother, I worked two jobs to pay my bills and placed her in daycare with the woman a few blocks away who had a rusty sign in her yard that read, "Daycare With Discount." I stole only a few moments with her early in the morning when I bathed, bottle-fed her, and dropped her off. Most nights, she was already asleep when I picked her up. I was home for only two weeks after her birth before I entrusted strangers with her wellbeing.

Now, at fourteen, she towered over me, cussing me out with an American accent, wearing shorts that I was certain made my deceased father turn in his grave. I stared at the foreigner before me. My mother died when I was in college. Struggling to make ends meet, I was unable to bury her. But when Rangarirai came into the world, a novel and miniature version of my mother, I was sure she had been reincarnated into this perfect gift. I named my baby Rangarirai, meaning remember. This way, whenever I looked at her, I would be reminded of my mother. I wanted my daughter to fill the hole of loneliness I felt in this country, yet that was too big a task to lay on her. I knew she needed my love more than I needed hers, but I was too broken to offer the best version of myself.

"You can't tell me what to do," she said as I ordered her to take down her Facebook page. Her friend's mother, who kept tabs on her daughter's profile, had sent me screenshots of Rangarirai's almost nude pictures and posts where she bragged about smoking weed. I was an awful mother for not knowing any of this, not even suspecting it. And that another mother had brought this to my attention was wrenching. I'd never even been on Facebook, and monitoring what my child did on the internet was too much trouble. After twelve-hour days or back-to-back eight-hour shifts, where was I supposed to find the time? I was happy when I came home and found her quietly locked in her room, "researching her homework" on the internet. I'd sit in the living room with a bottle of Chardonnay and empty it over the course of three hours.

In Zimbabwe, parents rarely made much conversation. They showed their affection by sending you to school, making sure you had all the supplies you needed, ensuring you were clothed, and getting you candy occasionally to spoil you. That was good parenting. Nothing more, nothing less. I had never told my daughter I loved her; we just didn't do that. My parents had never said those words to me, yet I never doubted it. Relatives, neighbors, and friends helped to instill discipline, unafraid to intervene with hiding if they caught you misbehaving. With an entire community taking turns disciplining children, there was not much left for parents to do. You do what you know, so I suppose I expected Missouri to do the same. Only America is a strange place where neighbors are petrified of disciplining the rascals next door. Instead, Rangarirai learned from TV shows, which I didn't bother to curate. Where I grew up, the national broadcast curated content for parents.

• • •

"Urikutvaga shamu. Ndinokurova!" I said with a stern voice.

"I'll call the police if you keep threatening to beat me. It's illegal, Mom," she responded.

I walked toward her, the wine whirling in my head, and lifted my hand to strike her. She picked up a stack of textbooks and blocked my arm. Infuriated, I shoved her onto the bed and pinned her down, my hands shaking in anger.

"Who prostitutes themselves at fourteen? If you're doing drugs now, what will be left of you at eighteen?" I said, forcing her to inhale my alcohol breath. "You're a disgrace to the nation. No Shona child does this! I swear, unenge unosvikirwa – demon-possessed. Remember, we are immigrants; you are not one of them. You are not an American."

"You keep saying that I'm not American, but that's all I know. I've never been anywhere else," she said as her bright red eyes stared at me.

The demon I sometimes witnessed manifest in her retreated, a helpless teenager emerging. She was right. *I* barely remembered what Zimbabwe was like, save for what I read in the news. How could I teach her what I didn't know? I could hardly afford to pay my rent each month, let alone two round-trip plane tickets. And, of course, no language learning app would ever have Shona to augment any efforts to teach her a new language. The guilt I often felt when I saw Mexican mothers speaking Spanish with their three-year-olds in the malls, when I saw well-behaved teenage Arab girls, clad in hijabs, speaking the language of their ancestors, flooded over me. I turned to face her, and my mother's eyes stared back at me in disappointment. I let go of her and lowered my head. I reached out to embrace her, but she ducked, ran out of the room, and locked herself in the bathroom.

"Open the door. Unopisa musoro. Let's talk about musikanzwa iyi, these obscene posts you're sharing," I said as I banged on the door. Silence. Let's see how long she stays in there, I said to myself as I walked to the kitchen to refill my wine glass, scraping mold off a patch of the wall right above the sink.

Police sirens rang outside as they typically did in my neighborhood at this late hour, except this time, they stopped right in our driveway. I looked outside and watched the officers leave their vehicle and rush through the rain. A knock landed on my front door. I held my breath.

"Rangarirai, what have you done!" I yelled as I pounded on the bathroom door. She didn't answer. I heard a second knock, a voice threatening to come in if I did not open the door. I walked over, reciting my story, and let them in. Only then did Rangarirai come out of the bathroom with exaggerated fits of tears. She asked for a social worker and begged them to take her away, reciting all the times I said Ndinokurova to her. She described how I had pinned her down, my drinking habits, and the times she'd had to defend herself from my raised arm that, in all fairness, never reached her. I cried as they took me to the station, the other car taking my daughter who knows where.

• • •

MY BREATHING ECHOED ON the walls. I paced my living room, searching for specks of dust nestled in the corners of the furniture. Noticing a light stain on the blue carpet, I rushed to the kitchen, wet a dish towel, and scrubbed until my arm hurt. The stain came out, but the water made it look like there was a larger, darker stain in its place. Frantic, I began drying the stain with the other side of the towel, but the doorbell rang mid-motion. I puffed out my cheeks and exhaled slowly, a faint whistling sound accompanying the release. It's been months.

Rangarirai stood behind a slender white lady, probably in her early twenties. This young girl was supposed to determine my fate? She herself was but a child, her arms covered in indecipherable tattoos with indecipherable shapes, her wrists draped in silver and gold bracelets, rings on all the fingers on her right hand, long, fake, pink nails. Buried in one nostril was a shy jewel. Iye wacho ainge anezvinomunetsa – I judged her. She introduced herself as Jane. I feigned a smile and invited them in, eyeing the damp spot on the carpet as though I would lose my child based on its presence alone. The day before, I had gotten rid of all my wine glasses, the wine too, even though the Cupcake Chardonnay had been on sale. Opening my arms, I invited Rangarirai into my embrace, but she clung to Jane and whispered that she was uncomfortable. I wanted to tell her, ndinokurova, simply out of habit but remembered that is what had gotten us here in the first place. Instead, I lowered my head and motioned to the empty couches.

Rangarirai pulled out the latest iPhone, the 11, and began typing away frantically. She averted my eyes the entire visit, speaking to me as though through an interpreter, addressing me by my first name, Fungai, instead of Mom. I looked at the social worker, waiting for her to admonish this rude behavior, yet she simply smiled and nodded, as though taking instructions from an adult who was capable of making her own decisions. I observed Rangarirai's new black and pink Nikes, with the swoosh facing the correct direction, her clothes a shade darker than I'd ever been able to buy her. Even from across the room, she smelled like fresh roses.

"Tell Fungai that my foster family is wonderful. My new mom understands me, respects my privacy. She would never spy on my Facebook account or read my diary. My new house in Overland Park is so big, and my room is so cool. Mom even drives me to school in a Range Rover. My friends are jealous! Plus, my little sister is totally adorable. I braid her hair for school. It looks just like Jane's," my daughter said, bouncing her head in excitement as she spoke. Again, she stared at Jane the entire time as though I couldn't understand her words and would have to wait for a translation. I felt my heart rot – kuora moyo chaiko.

Jane asked about my drinking problem, which was non-existent if you asked me. Sure, I went through a bottle of wine a few evenings a week, but wouldn't you if you had my life? She asked about my violent tendencies. Kuita here? – What tendencies? Had she been raised by my parents, she would know what a man's leather belt felt like on bare skin. She would recall the burning of her inner cheeks after a backhanded slap, the way her ears would ring as though infested by mosquitos, the way she'd have to hold on for balance to regain her vision. Perhaps that was my mistake. I never had quite disciplined her like we were disciplined back home. All I had done was issue empty threats. How foolish I had been to spare the rod, now the child was pure rot. I opened my mouth to speak, but words escaped me. I simply shook my head. Jane kept her eyes on me for a moment with an expression as indecipherable as her tattoos, then jotted something down in a notebook. I wanted to yank that book right out of her hands. How many of those notes were as fake as her nails? Instead, I swallowed my tears and chewed on my nails.

"How long does this foster family keep her?" I asked over the sound of my daughter's typing. Jane asked me to repeat myself then shut her eyes as though she needed to shut off the rest of her senses to understand my accent.

Before she could answer, Rangarirai turned her head and met my gaze for the first time. "I'm never coming back. They understand me and aren't always trying to tell me what I'm not. I can just be myself there," she said curtly.

I begged Jane with my eyes.

"We'll have to go to court. The judge will decide if you're a fit mother. It's going to be a hard case, given everything we've discussed. Plus, it's never easy for single moms working two jobs," she said in an accent that matched my daughter's. I felt like an outsider, invading Jane and Rangarirai's space. The remainder of the visit was a blur. Jane paced around the house, going in and out of rooms. With each door she opened, the shame of my Goodwill furniture grew, and my teeth sank deeper into my nail bed, removing a fresh layer. I imagined what this white family's home was like. Every Sunday after church, Rangarirai and I had driven through Overland Park, fantasizing about living in one of those houses someday. It was my fault. I had taught her that the life I provided her wasn't enough. I had taught her that driving luxury cars was what to aspire to, and now that she'd found this new life, she'd gladly moved on.

• • •

SLEEPLESS MONTHS PASSED. I spent my nights in Rangarirai's bed, smelling her clothes, cuddling her blankets. Sometimes I spoke to her as though she was right there; other times, I addressed my mother. Was leaving Zimbabwe for college worth it? I hadn't been able to graduate, completing only my first year before dropping out due to lack of funds. As the economy at home crumbled, my sponsor, Deltoid beverages, who had periodically offered academic scholarships, withdrew their support. I asked Jamal, my African American boyfriend, to marry me when I found out I was pregnant, not because I thought he would make a good husband or father.

Quite the contrary. I knew he would wreak havoc on us. He's the one who had introduced me to whiskey, wine, and vodka on those late nights in his dorm room. We both knew he wouldn't graduate with the drug use, which made his temper rage. He'd thrown a wine bottle to my face once, narrowly missing. I'd ducked as the glass shattered on the wall, sending large sharp shards across the room. I ought not to have been surprised at Rangarirai's behavior. She was, after all, half Jamal.

It was the need for that green plastic that had made me beg. I couldn't get deported, and marrying him would grant me permanent residence. We drove to Las Vegas, spending three days and nights in his 2001 Ford Taurus, eating Taco Bell and McDonald's, sleeping in mall parking lots along the way.

Jamal only saw Rangarirai once, a week after her birth. He said he wasn't ready to become a parent and would be moving back home to Georgia to be around his family and to regain his sanity. Despite my fears, he promised that he would ride out our marriage until I could become a citizen. Through the procession of diaper changes, sleepless nights, and warm baby baths, he soon became a faint memory.

When Rangarirai was five, Jamal showed up on my door, in a blue and white dress shirt, with a fresh afro mohawk. He had met a beautiful woman in Atlanta, and they were engaged to be married. He needed to finalize our divorce. I could tell from his voice, his demeanor, and his dressing that this wasn't the man I'd married. He had graduated with a Business Development degree and was working as an insurance agent. My heart ached. Why couldn't I have had this Jamal? I offered him wine, and he said he was three years sober. That's the first time I remember finishing a bottle in one night by myself while Rangarirai slept, locked away in her room.

Jamal asked that we keep our marriage quiet. He had never told anyone, including his fiancée, what he had done for a "poor African immigrant" in college. "It meant nothing," he said, as though reading my thoughts on the refined man he'd become and proactively curtailing any ideas I might have about a potential future together. I asked if he wanted to stay and meet his daughter. She was going to be home in an hour. He shook his head. "I can't even pronounce her name. I'm sure you're doing a great job raising her in your culture and all. I don't want to confuse her by claiming to be part of her but not being able to speak her language," he said, looking right into my eyes. He said it as though it were a matter of fact that our daughter would speak Shona. I wanted to explain that *she* couldn't pronounce her own name. Her R's were soft and sounded petrified like they were being chased out of her mouth. She hated her name and asked to be called Riri, like Rihanna. As the unworthy woman and terrible mother his presence reminded me I was, I signed the divorce papers and promised to never tell, even if Rangarirai asked about her father someday.

• • •

I STOOD IN THE courtroom, watching the pink, wrinkled judge in her black gown. I called out to my mother's spirit under my breath and asked that she and those gone before her help me to keep her namesake. Besides my daughter and me, everyone in the room was white. A well-dressed couple sat at the back of the room, holding hands tightly, bouncing their knees, and whispering. Mbavha! – These were the thieves buying my child's affection. If they only knew that she was all I had, they wouldn't take her away from me. Perhaps they would use their money to help me quit my second job and spend more time with her. Perhaps they would understand how my upbringing influenced how I behaved around Rangarirai. Perhaps they would find some unwanted child to love instead.

The judge's black robe was befitting of his role, a reaper whose sole purpose was to bring doom upon my life and that of my child. I watched the piles of paper on a side table, some cream, some beige, some new, some with crinkled edges, and wondered how many narratives had been written in this room, how many dreams splintered.

A fly zoomed across the room, landing at a window before struggling to escape, buzzing louder in frustration, fluttering its wings in desperation. I felt strangely comforted by its entrapment. I wasn't alone. There would be no happy endings for either of us.

The judge asked me to pronounce my name. I did, slowly, enunciating each syllable. She repeated after me, slowly and incorrectly. I lied, told her she said it perfectly. As she began to shower me with questions, she grimaced, her eyes closed as though in pain as she tried to decipher my accent. I knew I didn't sound credible, and my black skin didn't help either. To assuage her grimace, I began to reply in monosyllables, so my accent wouldn't be as evident. It helped. She relaxed somewhat. I turned my gaze to my baby, my eyes heavy with tears. To my astonishment, she looked back at me and forced a smile. The hearing remained a blur. All I could see was my mother staring back at me from across the room. "Please don't go, Mom," I begged silently.

As Rangarirai took the stand, I kept my eyes tightly shut.

"Hi, Judge. My mom hasn't really beat me. I was just mad at her for making me shut down my Facebook account," she began with a soft voice. I opened my eyes and looked over at her in disbelief.

The judge looked at Rangarirai. "You are safe. You won't be in trouble for saying what really happened."

The thieving couple covered their mouths and shook their heads like they were trying to dislodge them.

"I don't want my mom to get in trouble. There are some things she did that I liked," Rangarirai said, gazing at me.

"Like what?" the judge asked, skepticism drenching her gown.

"Umm, I miss hearing my name pronounced the way it should be like Mom does. I miss her cooking the food she says my grandmother used to make her when she was my age in Zimbabwe. Ummm. And she did my hair in mabhanzi – straightening it with thread; no one knows how to do my hair now. I haven't been able to find the right lotion either. One that doesn't leave my skin ashy, see?" the courtroom chuckled at her last remark.

The thieving couple's lawyer asked for permission to approach the bench. She whispered something, and the judge called for an adjournment.

Tears fell onto the papers on my desk, dampening the ink. I looked at the reflection of my mother across the room and said, "Thank you!" much louder than I anticipated. As we waited for the judge to return, I rushed into my mother's arms, with large dark brown eyes and soft features, and kissed her as Jane and the thieves screamed and lunged after me hysterically. I didn't care. I guess there was a part of her that was Zimbabwean after all.

Noon

Sekai

I caress the palm of his hand, yellow like the summer sun, and hope he's dead by noon. Beads of sweat form, swell, and burst, creating tiny streams across his face. His breathing is shallow, and he sometimes gasps as if being choked, slipping away. Don't be fooled, though. The old man must be scared of death; he holds on, struggling for every breath. He and I both know that hell awaits him. If only I could push him over.

I move my fingers through his silver hair, brushing it to the side, then lean over to kiss his forehead. Today is the first day he hasn't opened his eyes, quickening my hope. I wonder if he's still there. Does he know I'm here? The doctor said there is nothing more they can do; his organs are shutting down, and his jaundice will simply get worse. I trace the IV lines connected to him. In all their sophistication, they will do nothing to keep him in this life; they're simply here to ease his pain, the doctor said. I wonder if he would die sooner if he was in pain; perhaps he holds on because we made it too comfortable for him. I'm tired. I need to get back to my life. I can't be at this hospital for another today, tomorrow, and forever; I've already done that. I moved on, in my head at least four months ago when he first was admitted. I sit here because it's a worthwhile investment. The relatives can't point their fingers or cover their mouths as they whisper in each other's ears that his wife abandoned him at his dying hour. They can raise their voices and demand a piece of his wealth, *our* wealth, but hehe, watch me, Sekai, daughter of Mutetwa. I'll ship them his body so they can bury it as they please in that Zimbabwe. I've already googled California law; when he dies, all our property is mine, so nobody says pwe.

You know, I haven't always hated Zororo. After four years in Indiana, I was delighted to meet a Zimbabwean, to speak my language, and to reminisce about all things Harare and Shona. So what he was thirty years older? He understood me and saw me clearer than any Hoosier boy ever could. I said yes—yes to moving to California, to moving in, to his gifts, to the travel, to starting over in sunny Los Angeles, pursuing my graduate studies here. The MFA program, here I come! But soon after saying I do, I found his heart to be colder than an Indiana winter night, but my parents and uncles had squandered the roora he gave in exchange for me. I learned that I was simply meant to be a token to silence his relatives from their nagging about him never marrying despite being in his late fifties. I was the acceptable Zimbabwean muroora, one of childbearing age to pontificate the dzinza, an offering, though he never touched me in ways that could make me pregnant, only those that could remove a pregnancy.

I watch how miserable he looks and smile—for all those years he made my ears ring, for the times I cried until it was drought season in my eyes, for the times my skin turned purple from his discipline. I take my phone out and take a picture of him and send it to his relatives. "ZvavazvaMwari izvi," I write – Better to prepare them

for the worst. The monitors over his bed beep in the same monot-
onous rhythm they have had since the summer. I keep waiting for
them to hurry their pace, find their voice, and cry louder, then I'll
know reprieve has come. Or for the squiggly lines on the monitor
to jerk, scattering in confusion, but they seem as stubborn as him,
a reflection of his soul. Even the grass outside has begun to die as
the season changes, but this one, ah, hameno – who knows. I tap my
foot and bite my lower lip, turning to the clock that hangs crooked
above the door. The small arm of the clock, the lazier one, has decided to rest at the number eleven. Only one more hour until noon.

To pass the time, I google California theft laws. Zororo never
told me the full story about what transpired between him and his
brother, Pfumai, but perhaps if I sound intelligent enough, I might
be able to scare him away when he shows up. I scroll through pages
and pages of articles, learning about the process of pressing charges.
I'm not sure any of this will work, but I must be prepared to try
something. My phone beeps, interrupting what feels like thirty
minutes of searching. A text from Cole saying he has a surprise for
me, asking how long I'll be at the hospital, flashes across the screen.

"Hopefully no longer than an hour. I'm starving," I respond,
mentioning nothing about Pfumai's impending visit.

I wait for a response, but he doesn't text back; part of the surprise, I assume. Cole is the only good thing to come out of the last
few months. Pacing around the room, I wonder what the ratio is of
those who made it out versus those who died here.

I tiptoe to the hallway to make sure no one is nearby, then rush
back and slap Zororo as hard as I can. He doesn't move. For the first
time, I feel powerful in his presence. I am fighting back before he
dies. I can say that I didn't just take it for as long as he was alive.
Revenge stretches with me, making itself at home. I slap him again,
harder this time. Still, he doesn't flinch. His eyes remain shut, the
monitors beeping steadily, the lines constant. My eyes turn to the
IV bags; I cuss at them. I wipe the sweat from his face off my palm

on his bedding and then fold into myself in tears next to him. The ugly brother will be here with the lawyer at noon, finagling a way to get him to sign me out of his life. Maybe they will find nothing but a corpse.

Suddenly, large fingers grip my wrist with pressure so tight it feels like I have a sprain. I sit up in disbelief, my heart terrified and crouching in my throat, my body trembling. Our eyes meet. I search his face but can't distinguish between rage, fear, and desperation. He coughs, and the monitors begin to beep like I've wished for all along. Only, I seem to have breathed life into him. His grip is as strong as it was on those nights when he pulled my hair or landed his fists on me.

In a minute, a swarm of nurses rushes in.

"What happened, Sekai?" the youngest-looking one asks. I simply stare at them. He holds onto me as though his very life depends on it. Another nurse helps to release his grip on me. I retreat to the corner of the room. Beep. Beep.

Zororo mouths something, but the words come out crippled. I hold my breath. He stares at me, gasping for air. A skinny brunette affixes a breathing tube into his nose and presses buttons all over the monitor; the beeping stops. Slowly, he leans back into his bed but holds his stare. I wonder if he's sorry or angry.

"Oh, honey, sometimes patients just wake up. We don't always understand why. Don't be frightened," the brunette nurse says.

Yesterday I found emails from Pfumai to him and his lawyer, plotting to serve me divorce papers or something. Yes, the fat, ugly one who looks like he swallowed a hippo. I know that family. The roora they paid for me didn't bear them the fruit they desired over the ten years of our marriage, so now that he's dying, they're sending his brother, plotting on how to oust me from the inheritance. Now they regret pressuring him to marry a woman he never wanted, a woman who becomes the only next of kin that matters. I saw the lawyer's response that he didn't have a will, so it's all mine. Me!

I was the recipient of his anger and frustration; he took it all out on me before facing the world with his charm and smiles. Me—the one he paraded around as his beautiful young wife, showered with diamonds and kisses as observers bloated with envy at his façade.

I watch the clock. It's ten minutes until noon.

"I think he's stable—he's sedated," the skinny nurse says as they walk out.

I stop her at the door. "How do I get a Do Not Resuscitate?" I whisper.

She searches my face; I hold her gaze.

"Let me talk to the doctor," she responds softly before walking away.

What was this? Is he waking up? I can't have this! I'm not signing any divorce papers. I googled this. Even if he wakes up enough to serve me papers, if he dies before the courts can complete a judgment, the case is dismissed, and I'm considered a widow. Pfumai, the only family he has in the U.S., can't receive the inheritance instead. My husband can't rob me any more than he already has. I have dreams to achieve, more world to see, books to write, TV and radio appearances to prepare for once I'm a bestseller. I'm putting that MFA to good use. He can't destroy my spirit even in his last days. My freedom is near. Watch me rise, watch me soar!

Pfumai

It's not that I don't care that my brother is dying, but nyaya yacho MaOne! If I had gone to visit him earlier, while he was still lucid, surely, he would've recovered just so he could chase me away. Now that he's unconscious, I just have to deal with Sekai, that child of a woman he married. Given how much we paid for her, she couldn't even bear a child to carry our family name forward. I can't say I didn't warn them. You know the saying, Mukadzi mutsvuku akasaroya anoba – If a light-skinned woman doesn't dabble in witchcraft, then rest assured, she's a thief. In this case, I think we got both with Sekai.

Frank says that she's entitled to all the money as the spouse, and knowing her, she will not share a dime with us, his blood, not even our mother in Gutu. She was too clever in not having a child because then Zororo would have been sure to leave a will, and with money going to the child, it would be easier for us all to get our share. I'm clever, though. I knew that with that one, I'd have to stay ahead of her because she thinks she's smart. Manje, I found out that she is having an affair, sleeping with a child who barely got out of high school. Do you know you can get arrested for that? Once she knows that I have proof of her affair, I will get her to sign whatever I want. Wait until you see the look on her face.

I have been avoiding Zororo because of a small, small blunder from two years ago. I was in a tight spot, needed a job, and he recommended me to one of his friends, that black American rich man with a belly in Los Angeles, Dr. Brown. I was in charge of all incoming sales for his luxury car shop. Oh, you should've seen me in those days, driving around in a Porsche, in a Range Rover, even in a Bentley one time—me, Pfumai from Gutu. I started arranging deals, though, renting the cars out on the side at night, earning income, and putting them back in the showroom during the day. It was innocent; are you going to allow cars like that to just sit every night, not making you money until they're sold? Nonsense! I'm a businessman. I fixed all that. I got my own rental income on the side. I still sold the cars for the price he wanted and gave him his rightful earnings; his customers who bought their lightly used cars were happy with their new luxury purchases, and my customers were happy to drive the car of their dreams for an evening, impress the ladies—you know how greedy they are, they won't pay you any attention unless you pay up, flash a bit. It was a win-win-win-win if you ask me.

Business was booming, really. It was fine until those women in their short skirts with bums hanging out everywhere came to the showroom. I told you earlier, light-skinned women... There was a new Bugatti in the showroom. Yes, my friend, a real Bugatti, don't doubt me, I even drove it! I sent word out to my network that there were new wheels for rent, and the big bum ladies came, paying cash, twenty thousand dollars upfront for the night. I was so happy, swimming in money from one night of earnings, except... they didn't return the car in the morning, or ever. If I tell you how diarrhea can be induced by anxiety, you won't believe me, but it happened to me that day. Apa mudhara wacho, Dr. Brown was coming to town the next day to see his new purchase, imi! I took my twenty thousand plus the other thirty I had saved and ran, absconded into hiding. Ndaiitsanangura sei? – How did I explain myself?

Now, when Zororo found out about it from Dr. Brown, my phone would not stop ringing. It rang until angry, cussing voicemails filled the phone. Did you know that still happens even with these new phones? Then I blocked him when I found out the police were involved in the matter now; how do you sell out your blood? We are Shona! I've been hiding out in Texas ever since, keeping watch over Facebook with my fake account. I still called our family at home every now and then and explained it was just a misunderstanding between Zororo and me, but all was well.

Now when I found out that Zororo was ill, my mother tried to get me to visit, but I doubted it was safe. Now that he's dying, I can repay him by making sure that his wife doesn't steal from him. She knows nothing about the Dr. Brown matter. They hardly spoke in that house. Have you ever seen a couple whose misery is so very evident when you visit? Where you're afraid to take the next breath because the air feels rationed? That was them. Now I can walk safely into the hospital, tell her she needs to sign the papers, or I can tell her family back home about her boy-toy. I'll tell the world about what she's up to. The spy-man I hired to follow her before this visit said he had videos of them together, at it, in my brother's house too, imagine? I haven't seen them, but he says the boy looks like he barely left high school, a mere child. If I want the footage, it's a small fee. I'm telling you, if Sekai doesn't get in line today and sign, I'm posting those videos everywhere for the world to see. I'll fix her.

Sekai

Noon. The hippo walks in with Frank, the lawyer. I turn to the monitor; it beeps steadily, stubbornly. He isn't going anywhere.

"What are you doing here?" I bark at his brother. "You can't give a grieving wife privacy?"

"Pshh. You never loved him. You terminated all his pregnancies so you could live a blissful life and take his money when he's gone," he spews while still at the door.

I laugh. My husband's lack of touch made me doubt my womanhood, my attractiveness, and my worthiness. And second, so what if I live a free life and enjoy OUR money after he's gone? Are you so obsessed with the idea of the poor, suffering widow that the thought of thriving feels like sin?

"You laugh? Frank, you see this? The family was right. You're a witch! You're probably responsible for his failing liver. She laughs!" he says, raising his hands, his voice, and his eyebrows. He stands right in front of me, towering over me, pauses, and then rests his hands on his head in disbelief.

I take a step back and rest my hands on my hips. "I have cared for him for months when none of you bothered to be here. Surely you could've bought a ticket from Texas! I endured the last ten years with him, and all you reduce me to is a defunct childbearing machine? None of you have felt the pain I've felt. None of you care— you're all stepping in because you want his money," I say calmly, firmly before swallowing hard, tucking my rage down my stomach.

Pfumai approaches me and whispers in my ear.

"I know about your boy-toy, adulterous woman."

I fall into a stunned stupor. How? How does he know? We haven't seen Pfumai in years. He doesn't even live here. We've been careful, meeting only at my place, avoiding any public place until

Zororo was deceased.

"Haha! Right, wabatwa – you've been exposed. Raise your voice at me one more time; let's see," he says with a large, satisfied grin, four wrinkles forming from the corner of his eyes.

I feel my body warming up and fan myself with my hands, taking large, deep breaths.

"You know you could go to jail for that?" he says, his hands on his waist, shaking his head.

I scramble my face in confusion; what does he mean? Yes, he is ten years younger. Yes, he is Zororo's friend's son, but he treats me better than anyone ever has. He is respectful, asks intentional questions, and volunteers information about himself, his family, and his desires. I've never felt so cared for, so precious, and Zororo is as good as dead anyway. How was I supposed to handle this pressure all alone for months? With no family here, how do you think I coped? Cole was there for me, and you can't jail me for being in love.

Pfumai

Look at her; standing in silence and blinking like that will make her disappear. I motion to Frank to give me the papers. I will get her to sign now. Dzawira mutswanda – That was easier than I thought. We don't have much time. Zororo has lost his color, and he appears gray. He looks like an antique version of the man I grew up with. His eyes are deep-set into his skull, he has no cheeks, and thin skin lies over his cheekbones and jaws. If it weren't for the steady monitors, I would've assumed he is already no longer with us anymore.

"Is everything ok?" a voice says from the door. A young man holding a bag of Chick-Fil-A stands in the hallway.

I recognize his eyes immediately. I know him from somewhere. Rummaging through my memories, I attempt to place him but to no avail. Giving up, I turn my gaze to the lifeless man before us. But, like a puzzle piece finally falling into place, I realize that I know not him but a reflection of him, a ghost of sorts. Though, at first glance, he looks nothing like Dr. Brown, he carries his eyes. He is a muddled alloy of his father. From the way both Sekai and I gasp in terror, surprise at his presence, then shrink in shame, I realize one more thing. Sekai's boy-toy must be Dr. Brown's son.

The boy doesn't seem to recognize me. He never visited the shop while I was working, so we never met, and I'm not sure if his father ever showed him pictures of me after our little misunderstanding. I only assume who he must be because he is a mangled photocopy of his father. I need to get Sekai to sign these papers now and leave. His father might be behind him. But no, I reassure myself, these two have been going at it in secret. Dr. Brown is a dignified man. There is no way he would be ok with his son satisfying his friend's wife while his friend is on his death bed. I turn to Sekai and, sterner this time, command her to sign my papers or face jail time for being with an underaged child.

"He's twenty-five! He can date whomever he chooses. I'm not going to get jailed for that!" she barks desperately.

Sekai straightens her shoulders and walks toward me, a slow smile forming from the corner of her lips.

"You know who could get jailed though, if Cole called his dad and told him to press charges?" she says with a voodoo voice I have always known is within her, but she has never quite let out in this way.

How does she know? Sekai begins to laugh, softly at first, then loudly, like the possessed woman she is.

I turn to the boy who seems stuck in place at the door, oozing in confusion. If he keeps folding his face like that, he might dislocate it.

"My spy-man still has videos of you two in compromising positions. If you don't sign or call Dr. Brown on me, I will leak them online, then send them to your father!" I respond defiantly to her laugh.

Handitongwi nemukadzi – I will not be ruled by a woman.

Sekai

You've got to laugh. The nerve of this guy? He shows up like a vulture. At least I've been at Zororo's bedside for months. Gone are the days when I simply took the abuse, and this is California, fool; there are revenge porn laws out here that will *also* land you in jail. I know my rights. I smile at him.

Pfumai takes his phone out of his pocket and opens WhatsApp, gritting his teeth and breathing so hard his nostrils flare. He begins a video call.

"Here. Laugh in the face of the family, laugh in the face of his mother and siblings, laugh at us all – dzinza rese. Tell them every-thing you've been up to," he says, stepping back and facing the cam-era toward me. Slowly, familiar faces populate the screen of his iP-hone, forming a mosaic of boxes. I face them, stunned.

The physician walks in, a clipboard in hand and a pen in her white coat. "You asked for a Do Not Resuscitate?" she announces to the room.

The hippo and Frank turn to me wide-eyed. Pfumai takes the liberty to explain to the congregates on his phone what a DNR is. Wailing ensues. The physician looks at me, confused.

"Yes. I'm the spouse and the patient's legal healthcare deci-sion-maker," I respond defiantly, summoning my courage.

I hear my mother-in-law wail, then throw Shona cuss words at me that I thought she was too dignified to know. Pfumai charges at me, dropping his phone.

"I will tell everything! I will tell them all!" he yells.

I hide behind the physician. She places her clipboard between Pfumai and her. Frank rushes between them. Voices on the phone call out in distress. Frank tells his client to step away. Pfumai picks up his phone. "She's trying to kill him! Muroyi – Witch! Telling the doctors not to save him! Muroyi!"

Shaking, I step out from behind the physician. "Can you call security? Get them out and make sure they're never allowed back in," I say with a newfound boldness. Makadyaidzwa.

What do I have left to lose? Their minds are already made up. I've suffered enough. I won't let anyone control my life anymore. The physician scurries to the corner of the room and presses a button under the table. Soon, large men dressed in black rush in, flashing their badges. I point at Pfumai, at Frank, at the family on the phone. The physician nods in agreement. As the guards approach Pfumai, I turn to Frank.

"Go look up California Penal Code 647 and educate your client here," I say. Turning to Pfumai, we lock eyes. He holds my gaze.

"If you ever come back, *I* will put *you* in jail," I tell him.

Pfumai is dragged out, yelling obscenities at me. I cover my ears and search my husband for signs of life, signs of understanding, but find none.

A shriveled Cole walks over to me and embraces me, though I think he needs the embrace more than I do. He's clueless about what just transpired.

"What are you doing here? Was *this* your surprise?" I ask as I push myself out of his embrace, livid. The physician quickly asks if I'm ok, inquiring whether security should kick Cole out as well. I shake my head and gesture for her to hand me the clipboard. Pulling a pen from my purse, I sign the DNR, printing my name meticulously, using my married name for what I hope will be the last time. I look at the clock, twelve minutes past noon.

Torture In Minnesota

The first time you see snowflakes, they are big and fluffy. Like feathers of an albino peacock, they drift through the air as the light wind sways them from side to side. You decide heaven must look like this as you are mesmerized by the white carpet they create on earth. But, even in your wildest imagination, snow wasn't this stunning. You wipe the fog that's building on your window from your warm breath as you hear the excited chatter of your dormmates approaching your room.

Sometimes you feel like the freshman dorm pet, a ferret they collectively own, or perhaps some other exotic animal. Because you're from Zimbabwe, they take turns feeding you things. One day it's Puppy Chow—a Midwestern snack made of peanut butter and cereal; the next, it is Warhead's candy, as they all stare excitedly for your reaction to these firsts. Even though you constantly remind them that your name is Munesu, they often slip up, calling you Mufasa instead. You are expected to understand. After all, they're both African names beginning with "M." As you watch the season's first snowfall through your window, you know the approaching chatter is here to marvel at you as you touch and walk in the snow for the first time.

Picking it up, you scream in excitement, putting on the show they're here for, acting as though you're oblivious to the faces that surround you. Stretching your palms out, you attempt to catch the flakes as they fall, yet they disappear on contact. Your hands magically absorb the beauty, leaving you in chills. The cold is refreshing. This is the real America, you decide. Forget the sparkling water, the raspberry teas, and the laundry machines—those were all a farce compared to this. Phones click around you as your dormmates take pictures of you. Jacob teaches you how to make a snow angel, much to your delight. The crowd decides that sliding is next. It sounds fancy until you realize it's nothing more than mutserendende, the game you used to play in the village as a child. You and your cousins would climb up a hill in search of wild fruit, mazhanje, and glide down to the bottom on the red soil on your butts.

There are multiple pictures and videos of you on Facebook. You don't mind. This is an opportunity to brag to your Zimbabwean friends and family, proving that you are indeed in America and living the dream. One of the videos of you making a snow angel receives four hundred comments, some from Americans asking, "How has she never seen snow before?" But most are from Zimbabweans marveling at the beauty. They ask how cold it is or if it's soft. Mostly, though, they acknowledge their envy and complain about Harare's heat. It's summer down there. Over the next few days, a few more pictures are taken; some of the snow frozen over shrubs, making them look like ice sticks, and a few more of you in your snow boots, fresh from the Salvation Army store. They still feel foreign, as though you're wearing shoes for the first time. You pose in the coat you also purchased at the same thrift store. It's black and white, and the outside is itchy, almost like sackcloth.

After a three-hour night class that ends at eight-thirty in the evening, you learn the word blizzard. It had been sunny when you looked out your dorm window earlier in the day, so you were wearing flip flops and a cardigan for an expected slight chill. You are used to Harare's weather, where if you want to know what it feels like outside, you simply look out the window. You have yet to learn the deception and moodiness of American weather. You immediately recognize your ill decision as you leave the dorm, but you are running late and aren't about to give the Americans another reason to validate the stereotype that Africans are always late. You sit through a philosophy class, lost in the writings of ancient Greek scholars, warm in your seat as the central heating blows right above you. As class ends, you walk out into a furious and vengeful Minnesota winter.

The wind is cutting like sharp knives. You wrap your arms around yourself as it blows right through your cardigan, making you feel naked. Your exposed feet cry out for mercy as your toes become numb. The next building is only a few yards away; you run toward it but slip and fall, and your shoes have no traction. Stopping at each building along the way gives you twenty minutes to warm up before attempting another staggering dance back to the dormitory on the other side of campus. You begin to cry as you walk, but your tears freeze as though to spite you – Chando chacho chinenge chekutumirwa, kuroyiwa chaiko. Though the private college you attend isn't very large, it takes you three hours to get to your room. It had taken only fifteen to walk to class.

You've never cried about being homesick, missing your family, the tasteless cafeteria food, or not being able to express yourself in your language. Yet on this night, you escort the darkness away with your tears, crying straight through the night. Why would anyone choose to settle here if they don't *have* to, you wonder? You are in Minnesota because you received a full scholarship to study abroad. This is your only chance of receiving a higher education, but why do these wealthy Americans choose to make this their home? The snow feels like a lover you'd been infatuated with but was proving to be deceptive after you moved in with him. You regret the move; the domestic abuse is unbearable, but like most abusive lovers, they hold the power; you can't leave. All the while, Facebook comments occasionally trickle in on earlier winter posts. Your unsuspecting relatives and high school friends believe you're happy in this relationship, the luckiest woman in the world.

Over the months that follow, the white snow turns brown with mud as it is shoveled to the roadside. How unsightly. The ice remains merciless, ensuring that at least once a week, you slide and fall on your butt, regardless of the so-called traction your boots have. Perhaps it's because they are secondhand. The wind seems to cut right through your coat. Piles of snow along the road on overcast days make you feel like you're walking in gloomy, haunted tunnels. You count the days until winter's end, yet even after three months, it carries on. In Zimbabwe, winter temperatures are akin to fall in America and last only three months. You learn that it will take another three months before a reprieve from this frozen drudgery.

You have two jobs, one of which is across town, so you must wait for the bus that can be late and leave you standing outside for twenty minutes at a time. The other job is at the indoor basketball stadium on campus. You are to direct traffic at the gate, which means you are required to sit outside for four-hour shifts, telling attendees where they can and cannot park while they rush along into the heated building. Only the international students on scholarships work this shift. That's how you learn about thermoses and long johns.

You begin to walk around campus with a heavy blanket wrapped over your winter coat, without a care for the eyes that follow you and the giggles that sometimes ensue. As you enter each classroom, the blasting heat has you sweating like it's an angry summer day. First, you shed the blanket and the coat, then the hoodie, but you can't remove the onesie under your jeans and long-sleeve shirt, so you broil in the central heating. Can Minnesota make up her mind?

In Zimbabwe, you only owned two tracksuit jackets. There was no such thing as a winter wardrobe. This was all you'd packed for college. During the Zimbabwean winter, you sat outside and enjoyed the sun that was always present, despite it being shy and feeling like it was further away. You sat by the wood-burning fire and boiled maize, roasted nuts, and drank hot tea with milk. Here, you haven't seen the sun in at least a month. One of your dormmates watches a fake fire on TV while drinking coffee, which further depresses you. She says it psychologically makes her feel warmer. Your hair begins to fall out; a lack of sunlight and, therefore, Vitamin D, you wonder? Or simply a weird drying out since it feels more brittle. Your skin cracks, and no lotion will keep it moisturized. Only pure petroleum jelly seems to help.

As the fall season commences each year that follows, you have panic attacks about the approaching winter. Everyone proclaims their love for the trees that bleed orange unto their death. As they drink pumpkin spice lattes and dress up for Halloween, you feel the cloud of depression settle in. You can't bring yourself to appreciate the signs of the approaching doom, a doom that will last half the year. Your dormmates don't understand why you hate the winter so much. You want to tell them that it is only their privilege that allows them to enjoy it. They don't have to wait outside for the bus. They don't have to work shifts at the stadium parking lot. They all drive around with their heated seats and spend only a few minutes a day outside when they walk from a building to their car. Their coats are brand new, thicker, and better insulated. Some are even lined with fleece! And if they can't warm up, they spend five dollars on a drink to assist. If they are ever outside for an extended amount of time, it's usually because they have *chosen* to do so and can return to their heated cocoons whenever they please.

You're convinced that winter is the most deplorable thing that God has ever created. Hell ought to be cold because no matter how bad the heat got in Zimbabwe, it was never this unbearable. You move to Miami when you graduate four years later. In fact, you only applied to jobs in Southern states, even turning down a higher-paying offer in Maine that you secured after an on-campus career fair. Friends often invite you to go skiing or snowboarding, but you believe you've experienced enough snow to last a lifetime and can't understand why anyone would leave Miami, with its marvelous beaches, to play in the snow for a few days. It's been eight years since you've seen the horrid stuff, and you've sworn to never set foot anywhere where it exists again. You'll never be heard complaining about Miami's heat or humidity. You'll take the hurricanes, too.

Globe-Trotter

"**Y**ou can't wear that. You'll get us too much attention in the streets," my cousin says as she stares me down. I look in the mirror, confused. The red dress is knee-length.

"There's no cleavage," I protest, pulling at the spaghetti straps.

"Vanopona here nemagaro ayo. It's too tight," she says, laughing and grabbing my butt. "You can't get away with that in this part of Mozambique."

I grunt, rolling my eyes, but change into jeans and a loose-fitting, sleeveless yellow top.

She smiles in satisfaction. "They won't undress and shame you in the street like in Harare, but I don't want to deal with the whistling."

Stepping outside, I pick fresh mangoes from the yard. I wash off the dust and gooey liquid freshly-picked mangoes emit, slice them, and place them in the car. My cousin begins her tour, showing me around the city that she now calls home, munching on her mango slices.

We stop at Maputo beach. Stretches of bleached sand, punctuated with large puddles of water that reflect the sky, undulate. I take pictures of the island in the distance, the puddles so large they are almost one with the ocean. I'm startled to see so many black people at a beach. This much poverty and such idyllic scenery don't belong together. I expect the poor to be poor in the daily scenery available to them. Their eyes shouldn't be able to afford to behold such beauty. Though I'm in Africa, I expect to see mostly white people at the beach, swimming, surfing, and playing with their kids in the puddles. Is this damage caused by my years in America? Or perhaps by my British colonial heritage? It told me subconsciously that the finer things in life are reserved for the rich, the white. Zimbabwe, my home country, is landlocked, so I have no frame of reference, and the only time I was in the Caribbean, it was at a resort teeming with white tourists. The locals couldn't afford such views, such fine sand, such warm waters. Yet, here before me are black people, some with tattered clothes that haven't seen a wash in months. Couples hold hands, and kids chase each other in puddles, splashing and giggling. What a childhood, and what memories they're building.

My cousin says I must try the roadside grilled chicken. I hesitate but remember that I packed my Azithromycin. I'm ready to deal with a stomach ache. Besides, I'm in Southern Africa, exploring a country neighboring my birthplace. Whatever germs might be in the street food, better recognize that and have some respect. Makeshift tents with plastic garbage bags are tied to stick poles as a roof to cover the plastic tables and chairs on the sand. This is the best outdoor seating I've ever seen. The sun's rays lightly pierce through the plastic, and I bury my toes in the sand. My cousin speaks Portuguese, so she orders a full chicken and fries. We wash our hands with bottled water and dig into dashing flavors of garlic, unrecognizable spices, and bursts of lemon. As I chew with my eyes closed, I agree with her supposition; it's the best chicken I'll ever taste.

A fight breaks out a few tables down; I'm tense. She translates for me. They are vendors, and one has stolen a customer from the other. As she shakes her head and nonchalantly shoos men twice her size away, I notice an earring vendor in the distance. I'm a sucker for earrings.

"Don't speak," she instructs me. "We'll pay triple if they suspect you're a foreigner."

She motions for him to approach. I point to the ones I'm taken by, and she barters, haggles, then pays. I've been learning Spanish from a language app, and I pick up a few words when she speaks, mostly the numbers – tres, cinco. I'm reassured that my first solo trip to Ecuador will be a success. I'm content as I try on my newest possession, using my phone's camera as a mirror.

We walk into an ice cream shop, sit, and order. It's a modern store that mainly attracts tourists. The waiter speaks English and tells me I'm beautiful. I say thank you, then he responds by telling me that he's single and winks. I'm bewildered at his unapologetic flirting as he serves us. He asks for my number as we leave. I refuse to give it to him, yet he offers to comp our dessert. "Beautiful girl shouldn't have to pay," he says.

I know he doesn't own the place. He can't have the authority to make that decision, I insist. My cousin laughs because, to me, this is a moral conundrum. She pulls me by the hand, and we walk out without paying.

Ponto de Ouro is our next stop. A fantastic combination of red African soils and African markets lead to the beach. Vendors line the dirt road. Some sell fruit, others clothes, dried fish, and cooking oil. Each one is dressed in simple clothes that seem to have endured years of washing; some are barefoot. A table stall with a missing leg wobbling as a customer leans in to inspect the fruit. Again, I find myself thinking that the market is out of place, another lie that I've been fed; beautiful beachside properties are supposed to be excessively opulent, reserved for the rich, the white. We drive down the winding dirt road of soft sand-like earth. I remark to my cousin that I'm glad her car is a four-wheel-drive because we very well could get stuck. She tells me that the four-wheel was taken out, so though it looks like one, it really isn't. I'm not sure how that works, but I laugh. We drive for three kilometers to our lodging. It feels like thirty kilometers on this road. I wonder if there really is a resort at all or if we were scammed; there's nothing but sand and thick brush—no cars, no people.

A sign on the side of the road brings relief. We've made it. Carefully, we turn and drive up a steep hill, dodging rocks along the way to the reception.

The receptionist is a friendly, good-looking Mozambican, tall, smooth, dark skin, and athletic. He speaks English, which is not surprising as all the other guests here are tourists. He shows us to our tent as we chat. It hits me that I'd never met a Mozambican before this trip, even though my native Zimbabwe is right next door. I wonder what that says about my upbringing. A tent the size of a regular bedroom is perched on a hill, overlooking the ocean. It feels like I'm inside a postcard. The beach has light pink sand, and the ocean breeze blows fresh air into my face, sending my hair flying into the air. The receptionist is flirtatious, but I'm not having it. He says he'll come to keep us company at night if it gets cold. My cousin laughs. I don't find it amusing. The outdoor bathroom, built out of bamboo, has no roof and no door to shut. While showering, I can see the ocean and monkeys in the trees. I'm a little nervous about being naked out in the open, especially when the neighboring tent is a stone's throw away. Once I start showering, though, with the sun smiling above me and the wind serenading me in the steaming hot water, I know this is what dreams are made of.

Dinner is served under the stars. We watch the moon rise over the ocean, its glaring reflection blanketing the water. I order a traditional meal, Matapa. It's a mix of cassava, coconut milk, ground peanuts, and garlic, and it is to die for. As we eat, I get a text message from a Mozambican number. It's flirtatious, offering to come and give me a massage when I'm back at the tent. I turn to my cousin, furious that she gave the receptionist my number. She swears she didn't. I ruffle through my brain, then realize that he must have looked at my guest file; my booking confirmation had my phone number. I gasp in horror. My privacy has been breached.

"If this was America, I would sue the resort," I say, struggling to catch my breath.

My cousin lets out a dismissive laugh and shakes her head. "Welcome to Mozambique," she says, her arms wide open above her head.

Our dessert is served around a fire pit. We share thick, creamy baobab ice cream. Now the moon is right in the middle of the sky and looks like an ill sun. We sip on black tea, drizzled with milk, and huddle closer to the fire until our hair reeks of smoke. Before retiring to bed, we attempt to wash the smoke out of our hair. I wake up in the middle of the night. The tent is rattling. I hear the door's zipper in the wind. Is someone opening the tent? Oh no! That receptionist is keeping his promise. I must think quickly, but my eyes are heavy with sleep. I hold my breath and wait. No one comes in; the rattling continues. By now, I'm fully awake. I realized there was no one there; it was just the wind. Relieved, I go back to bed.

After three nights in the tent (with no unwanted visitors), we return to Maputo. I tell her I want African art to take back with me to my apartment. She takes me to an open-air market strewn with colorful paintings beckoning me to take them home from across the road. I look at her and tell her that this is where my life savings and I part. I want an African dress, but nothing that is too African or in your face, like West African clothes. After all, Zimbabweans don't wear those kinds of things, and I'm not about to start now just because I live in America. A halter-neck dress catches my eye. It's a bright sky blue with just a little African Ankara print in the center. It hints at being African but isn't shouting it from the mountain top. I'll get compliments because it's cute, but strangers won't stop me from telling me how much they love Africa or about their friend that has been to Burkina Faso. I also noticed a sculpture, a mother and baby Kudu intertwined, but I didn't know what I was staring at at first glance. Once the artist explains, it becomes evident, and I wonder why I had struggled to decipher it, to begin with. I know exactly where in my apartment it will sit. It's my favorite find of all my travels.

My paranoia makes me insist that my cousin helps me find malaria pills before I leave. I've had a mild cold since our stay in the tent, but she seems to call me every other month with malaria as though it's the common cold, so I want to be prepared in case my cold really is malaria, waiting to erupt. Luckily, the medication is available without a prescription. I love Africa for this.

Soon, it's time to bid my cousin farewell and leave on my first ever solo trip. Why Ecuador? Well, two reasons. First, it doesn't require a visa application for Zimbabwean citizens, especially U.S. green card holders. Second, I remember my lessons on Charles Darwin and how he came up with the theory of evolution because of how unique the fauna is on the Galapagos Islands. Since high school, it's been a bucket list item, but in a farfetched, dreamy sort of way. Now, as a grown woman, a professional living and thriving in the U.S., I can afford to just pick up and go where I want without so much as blinking at the cost. Mama, I made it.

The sculpture, a piece of home I must return to the U.S. with, turns out to be more trouble than I bargained for. It's heavy, so I must put it in my carry-on instead of in my checked luggage so that it doesn't count against my weight limit. It's probably better that way; it might shatter as airport carriers toss the bag around between transfers. But as I go through security, a Mozambican lady tells me that I can't take the sculpture on the plane with me.

"What can we do about that?" she asks as she searches my wallet and stares at a stack of one-hundred-dollar bills. I have two thousand U.S. dollars with me in cash. She smiles and calls over her colleague. They examine the bills and ask how much they are. I tell them. My stomach feels like it's leaking acid.

"Buy us lunch, something small," her colleague says. "Otherwise, you leave the sculpture here."

I don't have smaller bills, and the sculpture cost me twenty U.S. dollars. I'm not about to pay a bribe five times its cost. I tell them they can keep the sculpture. They exchange surprised looks, then the first one motions for me to proceed to the boarding gate. I pack away my wallet and leave the sculpture. She tells me I can take it with me. I smile. I won the battle without a bribe. Truthfully, though, had I had smaller bills, perhaps a five-dollar bill, I would have paid her.

As I sit at the gate waiting for my flight, I notice that the handful of white people in the terminal only chat up other whites, as though the blacks either don't exist or don't make for good conversation. An American girl in her twenties chats with an old white South African man. She lives in Washington, DC and is here working for an NGO, she tells him. Their conversation drifts to malaria. The American girl says that a colleague of hers in Ghana just died of the disease. He thought he simply had a cold. I've become keenly aware of the cold I have been fighting over the last few days. The South African man describes the very medicine my cousin bought me as the go-to drug for malaria. He says that he takes it as soon as he feels any symptoms at all because he can't gamble with the disease. The medicine is, after all, just a three-day course. I consider this to be fate. Perhaps God is trying to tell me that I must start taking my medication right away. I don't want to become deathly ill on a South American island. Immediately, I buy a bottle of water and begin the malaria course at boarding. It'll be tricky to figure out when to take the next dose, given I will be changing time zones soon, but I'm determined not to spend my time in the Galapagos holed up with fever and chills.

Usually, when I travel, I stay in an Airbnb. It's cheaper and feels more authentic. Since I'm traveling solo, though, my paranoia gets the best of me. I must be careful not to attract attention as a foreigner. Should I go with an Airbnb, my host will know that I'm a foreigner traveling alone. What if they send in a band of thieves for a young female in her early thirties? I decided to stay in a hotel and am quite pleased with my choice. It sits perched on a cliff. Other than my flights in and out of the island and my accommodation, nothing else is planned for the trip.

On my first day, I wander Puerto Ayora, the main town on the largest island of Santa Cruz. I speak only to tour operators, asking about what there is to do on the islands. I wander the fruit market, buying exotic fruit as it is my tradition whenever I'm in a foreign country. Sweet flowery scents fill the air. Fruit has always been my addiction. There's a quaint restaurant with a sign advertising margaritas for four dollars. It gets the best of me, and I order a passion fruit. I return every day for another for the remainder of the trip. I'm sure this restaurant will forever ruin margaritas for me. I find an ice cream parlor, ordering some freshly-churned coconut ice cream. At times, I'm impressed by my Spanish, but then someone says something I don't catch, and I feel like I don't understand a word. But what I know seems to suffice; people can understand me. After a successful first day, I go to bed with a full heart and a malaria tablet to hold me over until morning.

The first stop the following day is Tortuga Bay. I marvel at the beautiful sandy white beaches with giant iguanas sprawled over the beach. Every five steps, something catches my eye, and I stop to take a picture. A gentleman on the beach volunteers to take a picture of me with the beautiful creatures. I accept.

"I saw you yesterday at the fruit market," he says.

We chat briefly, and I'm on my way. My next stop is the Charles Darwin Research Center. I finally see the giant turtles that I have read so much about. They seem like living relics from the dinosaur age. I vaguely remember seeing a giant tortoise in my childhood. I was maybe three years old, at some park in Harare, perhaps even riding its back? The guide tells me that these are only found in the

Galapagos and Seychelles, an island off the coast of Africa. I could swear that my childhood memory is real, but the fact that I was riding the turtle makes me doubt myself. A local man chats me up, offering to take a picture of me.

"I saw you yesterday, drinking a margarita," he says. His friend nods in agreement. I marvel at the coincidence as we part ways.

The final stop for the day is the seafood market. Here, seals, pelicans, and iguanas congregate, begging in loud primal cries for lobster, crabs, and fresh fish that the fishermen are preparing to sell. The wildlife is mesmerizing. The smell of fish fills the air. A German tourist chats me up. He will be on the island for two days. He's cute and friendly, but he tells me that he misses his boyfriend. Bummer. He was a looker. Not that I would have given him my number or anything. Remember, I'm traveling solo; I can't risk being lured into any traps. Just quietly blend in.

"I saw you yesterday at an ice cream parlor," he says.

By now, I'm sure I'm being pranked. Why does everyone I speak to remember exactly where they saw me and what I was doing? I've been on the island for less than twenty-four hours. This is getting spooky. I google the number of people on the island: twelve thousand. I take note of what everyone else is wearing. Perhaps something about me screams tourist? But I'm dressed no differently from most of the girls on the island—denim shorts and a tank top.

The next day, I'm up early for a tour I booked to Isabella Island. The boat leaves at six AM. I'm at the harbor by five-thirty, but no one else is there. I walk around in the twilight alone, and at around six, a few people start to trickle in. There is no boat. Finally, at almost seven, the boat arrives. I'm mad that it's an hour late. I've been at the harbor for an hour and a half now. We take a bumpy ride that threatens to purge everything I ate last night. I'm glad I didn't have time for breakfast. You can tell who the Americans on the boat are. They shriek at each bump, shouting, "Oh my God! This is so bumpy!" as though the rest of the boat can't feel the bumps.

A gentleman seated next to me asks me where I'm from.

"Zimbabwe," I tell him.

He stares at me suspiciously.

"Where do you live?" he adds, hoping for clarity.

"Zimbabwe," I lie.

When I travel internationally, I don't tell people I live in the U.S. In case there's some scam to kidnap Americans for ransom or rob them because they're rich. No one is going to kidnap a Zimbabwean; it's not worth their time. My government will not be coming for me and will not pay a ransom. Besides, they'll probably assume I'm some poor African immigrant working manual labor, illegally, in whatever country I'm visiting. It's not uncommon to have someone offer me a job when I'm traveling in Europe, like the guy in Capri who asked if my cousin and I wanted to clean his house once a week after we told him we were from Zimbabwe.

"I saw you yesterday walking at the fish market," he tells me after he's asked how long I'll be staying on Isabella. I search his face, weird.

I spend the day snorkeling with sharks, turtles, and stingrays. It's the most immersive experience I've ever had. Despite the weird looks, I choose to keep my life jacket on when we explore the lava tunnels. It's a thirty-minute swim between canals. I can swim. I grew up swimming in pools in Harare but have never swum in rivers as most of them in Zimbabwe have crocodiles or Bilharzia, or both. Something is unsettling about thirty minutes of swimming in tunnels when I can't stop and stand on the ground or be at the shore in five minutes. I'm not sure about my strength and endurance either. Ignoring the weird looks, I keep the life jacket on and swim through the lava pools.

We stop to see some nesting Blue-footed Boobies on one of the lava beds. The guide tells us that the darker the feet, the more attractive the male. The young males, with lighter feet, must dance much harder to attract females. A male can dance for days and almost get the female, but once a male with darker feet shows up, the female ditches the dancer in seconds.

"I understand. It happens to all of us," a short, stout Swiss guy with a balding head says. I laugh louder than I anticipated, and the crowd joins me.

"Where are you from?" the Swiss guy asks with a smile. "I saw you yesterday at the Charles Darwin center." Hezvo! I give him the evil eye. This is sinister. He backs away.

After an incredible day of snorkeling, I head back to Santa Cruz. As I walk to my hotel, an Ecuadorian guy, perhaps in his late thirties, walks up to me. He introduces himself and says he wants to practice his English, so he attempts to speak to me but occasionally gets stuck and turns to Spanish. I want to practice my Spanish but occasionally get stuck and turn to English, a fitful dance. I rub my arms as a cool breeze settles in the late afternoon. He says he is a coffee farmer who plays music on the side and shows me a CD with his face on it. He reveals that the coffee farm belongs to his family. He wears a ponytail on the top of his head. The sides and back of his black hair are shaved but need a touch-up; they're overgrown. Although, he is tall and has a slim build.

"I saw you early morning at the harbor. Were you waiting for a boat to go to Isabella?" he asks.

I stare him down, then pick up my pace. This island has conspired against me! Whatever is happening can't be good. Tourists and locals alike seem to know my every move. I'm traveling alone, I'm trying to be discreet, yet everyone remembers my every move. He increases his pace, keenly aware that I'm upset.

"I'm sorry. Did I say something bad? Maybe my English come out the wrong way," he says, soft brown eyes echoing the sentiment.

I need answers, and he's going to give them to me, then I'm on the next flight back to the U.S. I pace back and forth, feeling my stomach roil. I wipe beads of sweat from my forehead.

"Your black skin is just so beautiful, so stunning. You beautiful girl. Hard not to notice on this island," he says as he reaches out to touch my arm, almost like he's seen a mermaid, a creature of legend.

He goes on about how he and his friends were talking about how unique I am. I laugh softly at first, but soon I can hardly stand. I clutch my stomach, gasping for air. Finally, I understand why the entire island remembers when and where they saw me. I laugh until he questions what it is he said that is so hysterical. I shake my head to motion that it's not his fault. I'm laughing at myself. I can't believe I hadn't noticed. Even though I'm on an island full of people I've been taught to call minorities, as I have grown accustomed to being called, there aren't really any black girls on the island, let alone ones as dark as me.

Imported Husband

He didn't know what a zip code was. Nor had he ever tried Greek yogurt, accustomed only to the runny stuff. Dudzai would need to teach Batanai what Walmart was, how to pay with a chip-embedded credit card, never mind Apple Pay. He would have to learn the difference between whole milk, two percent, and skim. She knew she would have to raise him as one does a child but cared not. It had been too long since she'd felt a man's touch.

They got married at nineteen, right after completing their A-level exams, before they understood the cruelty of time, that life never turned out like you imagined. No, she wasn't pregnant; she just loved him. But her parents assumed she was with child, that's why they accepted the roora without question.

She had first received a letter in her last year of high school at boarding school. He said he'd heard about her from a classmate who attended Zengeza 1 Primary School with her. Simply having the name of someone at the neighboring all-girls school was enough for him to pen a letter introducing himself and ask her questions about herself. Caging teenage hormones and isolating them in forested boarding schools without the opposite sex made for desperate overtures for a removed, foreign, exotic species. She found the letter from Bernard Mzeki, an all-boys school, a perfect escape.

They exchanged six letters over the three-month school term. Batanai asked about her dreams, made compliments about how beautiful she must be given her exquisite handwriting, included songs he dedicated to her, sprayed perfume on each letter, and signed off with SWALK – Sealed With A Loving Kiss. On Valentine's Day, he sent a card the size of her torso, much to the envy of the girls at school. By the end of the term, she was in love with a boy she'd never seen.

Their first meeting was during the April holiday break at Westgate Mall in Harare. He wore a Michael Jordan jersey, tan boots, a du-rag, and a neck chain that hung down to his belly button. It was as if he'd walked right out of an American rap music video. She was smitten. She watched him approach, turning impressed heads on the street. Their eyes met, and instinctively, they both knew who the other was. To impress her, he bought Wimpy burgers and fries to be savored outdoors. The conversation was harder in person, as though someone else had been writing his letters for him. But then again, she couldn't claim sole responsibility for the ones she'd penned either. Her replies were always a group effort, with her friends line editing and curating her thoughts. His eyes were more sociable and verbose than his mouth. They spoke of her beauty, caressing her ego.

After the meal, they went to the movies. He reached out for her hand. Although this was their first meeting, it was enough for Batanai to pen her a letter as soon as the second term started, declaring the love that ravaged him. Twelve letters, three more meetings over the August holiday, including another movie date, two walks around her neighborhood, then one more term of school, and he asked for her hand in marriage.

They attended the University of Zimbabwe as newlyweds, with her studying finance and history before she received a scholarship to complete her MBA at Columbia University in New York. They were happy during their time at UZ, propelled by the emotions of young love and their shared struggle with finances and daydreams of kinder days. He was supposed to join her in New York, but the US immigration system laughed at their plans. Ten years passed as she earned her MBA and then a Ph.D. in Finance, a postdoc. She was working at Goldman Sacks, her career soaring, when her green card was approved, making it easier to petition for Batanai to join her.

She knew it would be a disastrous reunion. She'd heard it in the way he complained that she didn't send him enough money. In the way, he casually gave her orders, as one does to a toddler. At thirty-three, what could she possibly have in common with a man she married after four dates and a few letters as a teenager? After one of their phone fights, she convinced herself she would leave him. There were plenty of men in America, all at the swipe of a screen.

But dating proved to be bewildering. First, she tried dating white men. But her large behind and curves, which had been the envy of all women and the desire of men in Zimbabwe, were a liability. White men preferred the skinny mabhonzos she and her friends used to tease in high school for their lack of shape. Dudzai found herself forsaking sadza, rice, and other foods from her childhood, hoping to shed a few pounds. She held contempt for her mother, for the boarding school, for the entire Zimbabwean community, for nourishing the lie that a fatter woman was more attractive. She ate only salads and cans of Progresso soup, yet the flesh clung to her pelvis, to her abdomen. She comforted herself by telling herself that she had never been attracted to white men anyway. What's one to do with all that ghostly paleness?

Next, she tried dating African Americans, all that melanin, and someone to talk about the black experience with, but she never felt understood; their cultural differences were too extensive. They couldn't even seem to agree on what constituted racism. She turned to African men, yet they, too, seemed to prefer women from their own countries. Nigerians wanted someone who could make egusi soup and jollof rice, Cameroonians wanted someone they could express themselves to in French, and South Africans thought they were above Zimbabweans. What was she to do? Batanai would surely be a burden, but at least she would have someone to share a bed with, someone to speak to in Shona, someone who wouldn't need her to translate her jokes, making them lose their meaning.

"Ndiisire muboora. I want pumpkin leaves. This other food you make is tasteless. You've become a bad cook," he said to her on his first night in New York. She tried to explain that the food in America didn't taste the same; none of it was organic and freshly picked each morning. Besides, where would she find pumpkin leaves for sale – kanandimiwo?

Batanai had been a teacher in Zimbabwe, and teachers she knew all too well from her mother felt like they knew better than everyone else in the room. It was hard for them to switch their brains off and realize that they were out of the classroom context where they were the smartest people, and everyone didn't need to pander to them for gold stickers now that he was in New York. He continued to teach her at every opportunity, whether it was about buying a home, even though he didn't know what a credit score was, or about how she ought to clean the carpet when he had never laid eyes on a vacuum cleaner.

Dudzai's first goal was to help him get a job, but Batanai refused to drive for Uber; he didn't want to become a hwindi in America, he said. He wouldn't work at any fast-food place because kitchen work was for women. Being a cashier or stocker was manual labor, and he was a professional. He insisted on a fancy job like hers, but she was far much more educated than he; still, he put sticks in his ears. When Dudzai suggested he return to school and earn his certificate in teaching African History in the US, like he had done in Zimbabwe, he refused, insisting on a career upgrade.

"I'm the head of the household," he often asserted whenever she suggested something. She found that ironic, given that he had to ask her how to lower the volume on the TV.

As the winter approached, their relationship became colder and colder. Dudzai came home to find a new car in the driveway.

"I bought it for you!" Batanai exclaimed. Dudzai searched his face for a sign of jest. She felt her palms get warm, then clammy. She charged at him, stopping dead in her tracks as he opened his arms for an embrace. She had added him to her credit cards to help him build a credit history. Feeling rich with a fifty-thousand-dollar credit line, he decided they needed a brand-new Mercedes. Dudzai took a deep breath, unsure of how to feel. On the one hand, he had tried to do something for her, but she was the only working spouse and would be the one to pay off this extravagant purchase.

"We need to drive a car that shows you are a Wall Street woman," he said as he pulled her into an embrace. She heaved loudly, blinking back tears of defeat.

"Bho here sistren?" he asked after seeing the expression on her face. She wasn't as excited as he had anticipated.

She nodded and placed her head on his shoulder, listing in her mind what would need to come off their budget so they could keep the car, then promptly added it back, knowing how he would react.

• • •

"DUDZAI, I'M AT THE front desk. Tell this woman to let me in. I told her my wife works here, but she says you need to come and complete the visitor sign-in," Batanai said as he tapped his foot. Dudzai felt her stomach drop. She pulled her leather chair away from the oak conference table and walked out of the work meeting, whispering apologies on her way out.

"You're not allowed inside. It's a rule. The guard didn't know what he was talking about. You need to go home, otherwise, I'll get in trouble," she lied as she pulled him aside, lowering her voice and looking around to see if any of her coworkers had seen him. Earlier in the day, she had arranged for him to get his teeth cleaned, and the driver was supposed to drop him off at home, but instead, he had insisted on getting dropped off at her office. She stared at his outfit in horror. He still dressed the way he had on their first date, his taste never evolving, stuck in the past. She gave the security guard her home address and asked him to escort Batanai down and hail a taxi for him. As they walked toward the elevator, past the elephant ear plant, Dudzai exhaled in relief and walked back through the glass doors.

"Who was that?" her red-haired colleague asked with unwelcome delight.

"Nobody," she replied, and she walked back to the conference room, head held high with a face of stone.

It wasn't just Batanai's fashion sense that had remained stagnant. Dudzai didn't want to go to the movies for dates anymore, preferring instead the symphony, a Broadway show, the ballet, or the Met, all of which he believed to be a waste of time and money. When she tried to take him out for date night, he wanted to eat at McDonald's or Burger King, comparing them with the fast-food restaurants back in Zimbabwe.

"You're trying too hard to become American," he would warn her when she said she would rather try New York's Michelin-starred restaurants.

She looked at his wannabe rapper outfits and, in those moments, wanted to say, "What about you?" Yet she knotted her tongue, knowing it wouldn't be long until he uttered, "I'm the head of household."

• • •

THEY SAT ON A sunny restaurant patio in the West Village on a Wednesday afternoon lunch break, Dudzai's compromise for not having him in the office. She knew trouble was imminent when she noticed her boss wave from a distance, his teeth on display and delight in his eyes. Please don't say anything about me bringing him to the office, she prayed. She got up, and her boss embraced her and kissed her on the cheek. Batanai stood up and asserted firmly, "This is my wife."

"I didn't know you were married?" he said as he faced Dudzai. "You have a jewel of a wife in Dudzai. Such a beautiful and smart woman," her boss told Batanai.

He pronounced the D's in her name as though his jaw was dislocated or he'd just had his wisdom teeth out, and his mouth was still numb from the lidocaine. Dudzai carefully directed the conversation around the weather and sighed in relief as he told Batanai it had been a pleasure to meet him. But as her boss turned the corner, Batanai turned to Dudzai, his eyes wide open, and banged his fist on the table.

"You're kissing your boss? You don't even tell people you're someone's woman? He dares to call you beautiful in front of me? Are you having an affair, Dudzai? Is that why you wear all that makeup and spend so much time getting ready in front of that mirror each morning?" he said, flipping their burgers onto the floor and storming off, the veins in his eyes visibly filled with a rush of blood.

She sat alone, watching the cars drive by, the couples holding hands and kissing, and shook her head in disbelief. How was she going to bridge the gap time had cruelly carved out between them? There was no returning to the dating pool; she knew what awaited her there, but, she wondered, could an equal measure of time also bring them closer? She waited longingly, looking at the corner where he had turned in the hope that he might return.

After fifteen minutes, Dudzai walked back to the office. As she approached the glass office building, she heard a familiar voice cry out, "I need you to take me home." He didn't know how to use the subway system, didn't know how to request an Uber, and certainly would get lost trying to navigate the streets alone. She ordered a taxi.

That night, when she got home, he sat in the center of the living room with arms folded over his lap. "It's time to have a child," he told her as she walked in. "We begin tonight," he ordered as he made his way toward their room. She knew it was because he felt threatened by her boss. In his mind, what better way was there for a man to mark a woman as his territory than to have her walk around, evidently bloated from his semen. She was already raising one child, so what was one more, she convinced herself. Besides, the joke would be on him. She could use him to satisfy her cravings, making up for the decade of deprivation.

A year of trying came to an end with no result. She watched as new months ushered in blooming flowers in Central Park, but they aged and died in the summer heat. Bright yellow leaves, which turned orange before their death, sprouted, and a chilling wind soon whistled across the city.

• • •

SHE FOUND THE MUPOSTORI in their living room with a bucket of what looked like skim milk. He was a Zimbabwean man who lived in Texas and came from a cult that wore only white robes. She eyed his freshly shaven head and overgrown beard. The sect conducted all-night prayers in the mountains and claimed to be able to see the supernatural and predict the future. "I thought all the Mapotsori were all left in Zimbabwe?" she joked. Batanai gave her a disapproving eye.

"Ah. Here, wash in this water. Remove your clothes so I can pray for you as you wash," he said with a voice that rumbled. She cringed, afraid the neighbors would hear them. Dudzai eyed her husband, awaiting the anger that had become her closest companion. Instead, he nodded for her to obey. Matakanana chaiwo. She realized why Batanai had gone out of his way to find a Mupostori who could help them cast spells to get pregnant; he was still trying to prove his manhood because of a stupid encounter with a man who wasn't even in her life anymore, a former boss who had since moved to Merill Lynch.

"You have a problem with my boss, but are you fine having another man stare at my naked body?" she wanted to say. Instead, she asked to bathe in the bathroom and have him pray through the door; after all, the spirit was everywhere, she insisted.

The Mupostori was quiet.

She took a stab at his ego. "I hear the best of you can even heal over the phone."

With that, he nodded his approval. She dumped the water in the bathtub as they chanted and prayed outside the door. She sat fully clothed on the toilet seat and read the *Essence* magazine she had left on the stool. As the men raised their voices, clapped their hands, stomped their feet, and made other unintelligible sounds, Dudzai removed the broken tile in the corner of the bathroom and took out her birth control, popping each pill out of the sachet and dropping them in the toilet before flushing and putting the tile back in place. Batanai couldn't know. She laughed silently to herself at the hysterics of the healer. When they completed the prayer ritual, they requested she come out, so she doused herself with a wet towel to give the illusion of having bathed in the milky water. Mupostori laid his hands on her, then jumped into the air to catch zvishiri, evil spirits, wandering off to the door like a madman, almost running into walls. Dudzai imagined him packing the demons back to Texas with him on his carry-on, the spirits setting off TSA alarms and finally possessing unsuspecting infants and toddlers on the plane, much to the misery of their parents and unsuspecting passengers. Perhaps, when he landed, he would leave them for some other unsuspecting Zimbabwean victim, so he could be hired for another exorcism. She tried not to giggle at the thought of birth control demons.

Batanai pulled her aside as the Mupostori packed up. "You need to pay him before he leaves. I promised him airfare, a hotel stay, and another three thousand for his troubles. It'll be five thousand altogether," he said.

Her blood curdled. This was her hard-earned money! Batanai was annoyed that she did not have the cash right on hand. She couldn't withdraw that amount from the ATM, so the Mupostori would have to wait till morning when the bank opened, and she could walk in. Batanai apologized profusely to the prophet. "You know, women, it's like instructing a child. They can be brainless sometimes," he said. She lay still through his thrusts that night, which were accompanied by prayer chants that mimicked the white-robed man.

Yet another six months with no pregnancy.

• • •

"Guess what came in the mail? You have a work holiday party with your spouse to go to, huh?" Batanai said excitedly. She had decided against attending. She just wouldn't mention it at home, yet they had sent out formal RSVP requests in the mail. Batanai opened all the mail, though nothing was ever addressed to him. She knew it would only be trouble bringing her backward husband into her circle of sophisticates, but perhaps more trouble for her to refuse to attend because, surely, he'd try to attend without her. Dudzai had mastered living in alternating identities. The strong, high-powered, and respected woman at work, yet utterly voiceless at home. She knew how to cope in each world, but bringing them together was a skill she had yet to master.

This time, she dressed him, took him shopping, and taught him dinner table etiquette. No chewing your bones and sucking the marrow. She fed him lines that would make for appropriate small talk and warned him about sharing more information than necessary. As much as Americans asked questions, they didn't really care to know the answers, even when they ask how you're doing, she explained. She was hopeful that as long as she kept him largely silent, speaking only to ask the questions she'd fed him, she could survive the night.

"How come you only work with men? I'm not comfortable. We need to get you a job where more women work," he whispered as she introduced him to her coworkers and their spouses.

She wanted to rattle out the statistics of female executives on Wall Street, but instead, she responded, "Let's just have a good time tonight."

As the wine dwindled, attentive waiters eagerly refilled any glass slightly below half, making it impossible to know how many glasses one had truly had. The conversation soon centered around Batanai, her coworkers asking what he did for a living. He puffed his chest and spoke in his clunky accent, "I have lots of businesses in Zimbabwe. In fact, I make more money than my wife. I'm the breadwinner, providing even this dress she is wearing, even the underwear underneath," he said.

Light laughs followed her colleagues and their spouses, unsure whether this was a joke or not, given his straight face. As Batanai continued his banter, she saw their past unraveling before her—the letters they had exchanged in high school, the four dates before their marriage, their blissful college years, and her time in graduate school in New York. They had both become products of the societies they lived in. She stared at him as he tugged awkwardly at the handkerchief she had meticulously folded into a square pocket, boasting about the car he bought her and their plans to have children—only boys, for he had no use for daughters! After chastising her older and stubborn womb, Batanai snapped his fingers at the waiter across the room and waved his empty wine glass at him.

Dudzai grabbed him by the arm and pulled him to the lobby. "You're done for the night. We're going home," she said as she dragged him out the door.

"I was the alpha male in there," he said to her, clearly intoxicated. "Ndivo vakadzidza vacho ava? – I'm smarter than all those men," he added.

As they walked out, his chatter was punctuated by the click of her heels on the tile, car horns blowing in the street, and sirens fading away into the distance. She clutched her coat tightly as the December windchill of New York cussed at them. "We're getting a divorce," she asserted without looking at him as the valet retrieved the Mercedes. Dudzai felt her pulse in her temple, her body heat in her ears. This was an order, her order.

Not So Micro

I followed her down a tree-lined street, nodding my head to her excited chatter about how deep these people were, how big their hearts were, how welcoming their demeanor was, and how excited she was for me to meet them.

Maddy and I had been introduced two weeks prior at a fundraising event for newly resettled refugees in the San Francisco Bay Area. We hit it off when we realized we worked for the same hospital. We exchanged numbers, and a week later, she texted, inviting me to her friend's housewarming party in Palo Alto.

The front door was propped open, and Maddy walked in, gesturing for me to enter the dining room. I watched as red wine sparkled in loosely held crystal glasses around the room, grateful to Maddy for bringing me into her fold. Besides Maddy, I knew no one else there. I listened to the excited chatter around the room and the laughter that filled the air. I eyed the table full of hors d'oeuvres. I found an opening between two women, probably also in their early thirties, and shifted my weight to squeeze between them. Maddy hugged everyone in the room, giving compliments to each person before moving on to the next. She settled next to a tall white guy in his late thirties, Zach, a Director of Engineering at Salesforce.

"What's your name?" he asked me with his arm extended in greeting.

"Tariro," I responded with a coy smile. Even from a distance, I could smell his cologne. I could tell he was the type that probably spent two thousand dollars a month on a personal trainer and another six hundred a month on a gym membership. He wore a black Patagonia jacket, but I could tell that beneath the layers of puff lay well-sculpted arms.

He squinted and nodded, daring not to repeat my name back to me as he had upon introduction to every other guest.

"Just call her T," Maddy said. I heard a sigh of relief from everyone in the circle.

Giving Maddy the side-eye, I addressed everyone. "Please do not rename me. Tariro is just fine." The relaxed atmosphere tensed; the shift was visible in everyone's limbs. Lips were folded inward, ears scratched uncomfortably, and fingers fidgeted across the room.

"This is a nice house. Who's the host?" I said to ease the discomfort.

I learned that Zach and three other guys were renting the house for eight thousand dollars a month. Each one had their own bedroom, but the house had only one bathroom. The old, musty smell was a stark contrast to the new gadgets, most of which I could not identify, that graced every room. Zach reached for a bottle of Syrah, and two almost empty glasses were immediately raised. He refilled them both, then drained the bottle into his own glass, fidgeting with the cork in his left hand.

"Where are you from? I have a friend from Asia who came to study in the U.S., and she just gave herself a new English name because hers was too hard to pronounce. You should consider doing the same," Katie, a redheaded Facebook recruiter, said.

"Zimbabwe. You can learn how to say my name. It's fine if you don't get it right the first time, but please try," I responded gently, with a feigned smile.

At the mention of my country of origin, a few of the women in the group exchanged knowing looks and whispers.

"We should hook you up with Feye. He's from Kenya. You guys will have the cutest babies!" Katie said.

I'd heard this all too often. Each time someone in Silicon Valley told me they had just the *perfect* blind date for me, it was with the only other black person they knew. It was as if character, personalities, and interests mattered not. To them, I was black and he was black, so that meant we had to be a match, right? This bewildered me. I would never think to set up my friends because they both had blue eyes.

I smiled. "That won't be necessary," I responded.

"My friend went to Nigeria a year ago. It looks beautiful out there," Zach said, staring at me intently for a response, his eyes bright and teeming with fascination. I wanted to tell him that Zimbabwe was just as far away from Nigeria as Japan was from California, that just because the two countries were on the same continent didn't mean they had much in common—the landscape, the language, the culture, the food were all different. I'd never been to West Africa, and it sounded just as exotic to me as I'm sure it did to him. Dofo!

Zach pulled out his phone and showed me his Instagram account.

"This is me with a bunch of kids in Guatemala, building houses. I love helping people from poor countries whenever I can," he said. He paused and zoomed in on the picture.

"My hair looks a bit overgrown in this one—maybe I should delete it," he added.

I watched as the others cooed over how cute the barefooted children were. They commented on the darker hue of their skin, their heads of full black hair, and their tattered clothes.

"You know," Zach continued, "I know someone who owns a restaurant who would gladly hire you if I put in a good word for you. That's what I love about San Francisco. We accept *all* immigrants. Don't worry about not having documentation; he doesn't care."

The circle of guests gasped at his generous offer. Women put their hands over their hearts and titled their heads in anticipation of my reaction. I felt my ears burning as I picked up my glass of Pinot Noir, ndokundidhokonyaka uku? – He's trying me.

"I'm a physician at UCSF," I said between sips. "I don't need a part-time job. I'm also a permanent resident, so don't worry about my documentation."

They all stared at me, unsure of whether to laugh or apologize. I didn't help them decide. Their half grins made them look like they were in pain.

"Have you ever had honey ham?" Maddy asked me, trying to change the subject. "It's so good! You should try a piece," she said as she cut a piece from a platter on the mahogany table. She picked up the slice and held it toward me.

"I've been in the U.S. for fifteen years. I know what it tastes like. I'm not a fan, though. Thanks for offering," I said.

Slowly, everyone retreated to the living room, leaving Maddy and me alone by the table. She stared at me, regret in her eyes, and I read the look with clarity: she wished she hadn't invited me. I joined the others around the eighty-six-inch LG flat-screen television, clenched my wine glass, and sat in the only remaining seat next to Katie. I took a deep breath, then a large gulp of wine. At least the wine was good, I told myself.

"Is that Africa's real hair?" Katie whispered to a girl whose name I didn't know. I felt Katie's arm reach for a few braids. I shrugged her fingers off; kuti zvidii?

"Please don't," I said, without attempting to be polite. She stared at me as though trying to ascertain without touching it.

"Does your skin burn?" she asked as her eyes scanned me from head to toe. Normally, I wouldn't mind such a question, but my annoyance with her was blooming oh-so-beautifully. The wine probably didn't help either. I gave her the evil eye and ignored her, turning my attention to the screen. Maddy walked into the room and stood in the corner next to Zach. She turned up the TV volume and glanced at me with determined confidence. She wasn't going to let me ruin the evening. We watched as Andrew Yang made his announcement to drop out of the presidential race.

"I could never date an Asian guy. They love me, though," Maddy said as she stared at the screen. A few girls echoed her sentiment, chiming in on why Asian men were so unappealing.

"I love his policies, though. Democrat for life!" Maddie added as she played with her ginger locks. I rolled my eyes – kutinyaudza.

"Well, that's why we all moved away from our ignorant, racist families in other parts of the country. San Francisco is the only place that treats people equally and carries no bias," Zach said.

I chuckled. After taking another gulp of wine, I reached for my phone and opened the Uber app, picking the more expensive option because the driver was only five minutes away.

"So, I heard that in Africa, everyone has big families. How many siblings do you have?" asked the blond-haired roommate.

I wanted to tell him that I grew up in an affluent suburb in Harare, not in a National Geographic village, that my mother was a pharmacist, and my father a finance manager. I wanted to tell him, yes, I could swim before he even asked. They always asked. I'd grown up in a house with a pool in the backyard, in a home much nicer and bigger than any home in Palo Alto.

Instead, all I said was, "one."

A notification flashed across my phone; my ride was a minute away. I smiled and took the last sip of wine in my glass.

"I have to leave. Early day tomorrow," I lied as I got up. Maddy looked at me. She knew I had the week off; we had just talked about me resting over the next few days. Work was going to be awkward if I ever ran into her again in the cafeteria.

"Bye," was sung in unison as I approached the door, the oak floors creaking with each step.

"Did she seem a little uptight and angry to you?" I heard someone whisper as I cracked the door open.

"Black women are always angry," Katie whispered back as I shut it behind me.

I stood outside and looked up at the sparse sky, dotted with but a few stars, drowned out by the city lights. After zipping up my jacket, I breathed onto my fingers to warm them up. A ravishing young white man with a well-manicured beard drove up.

"What's your name?" he asked, looking at the directions that populated the screen of his white Tesla.

"Tariro," I responded.

"Oh, that's too hard. I'll just call you T," he said as he drove off, chatting away into the dark. I smiled, picking my battles – chikuru kufema.

It's So Much More Complicated When You Love Him

Our feelings for each other exploded in the most unlikely of places: a set of stairs in the entryway of a mall. Traffic into the mall was scarce, but the floor was as filthy as you would expect. We cared not; something larger was in labor. I followed the way his blond beard traced his face, his lips. I noticed the tiny wrinkles that formed in the corners of his eyes when he smiled. We may as well have been sitting on a white sandy beach with turquoise blue waters, feeling the caress of the sun, oblivious of Kylie.

We had met six months ago through mutual church friends, and though the two of us had never hung out alone, we spent enough time in a group setting. I'd watched him from the corner of my eye, listening to his commentary on the political climate with approval. On this night, the movie our group of friends was supposed to see had sold out, and, for some reason, instead of going home, he and I, along with Kylie, lingered.

In hindsight, I think it's the spark between us that made the three of us stay and talk for hours. My curiosity with him, his with me, Kylie's with him, too. I watched her twirl her hair and lean into him, complementing his fresh cut in a voice so low, she sounded like a frog was stuck in her throat. Zvipiko, I rolled my eyes. She wasn't being sexy. He was far too sophisticated to be entranced by this foolery.

"Are you coming down with a cold?" I asked Kylie, with sarcasm crouching behind concern.

He laughed. I smiled. Perfect chance to reel him in.

"Have you been following the crisis at the border?" I asked. His face lit up as he turned to face me, giving Kylie his back. I glanced at Kylie, who was shuffling her fingers like a deck of cards. He looked at me, his face animated, his hands waving in the air with passion. He was hooked.

"Kylie, what do you think?" I said, inviting her back into the conversation, pretending we were all friends.

It was clear he was paying more attention to me, asking me more questions, then occasionally turning to Kylie as an after-thought. He asked about my childhood in Zimbabwe, about the transition to college in Louisiana, about my hobbies, and my career. With each question, he met my eyes, wrestled them in a stare, then defeated me with a smile as I timidly turned away. The security guard approached with orders for us to leave. Kylie asked him for a ride home, though she very well could have asked me. He agreed. I hugged him goodbye. I wasn't worried.

As I drove into the dark that night, my heart swelled. One moment, I was convinced he liked me, then I wavered, certain he was just curious about my African heritage. Then I spiraled, wondering if he'd spend more time with Kylie when he dropped her off. With each car that zoomed past my red Honda Civic on U.S. 101 South, I formed a new supposition of his intent.

I had been curious about him, but after this evening, a flame had been set ablaze. I started with Facebook to see what else I could learn about him. I already knew he was a technical product manager at Google, was born and raised in Montana, and had moved to California for his career. I scrolled through his pictures, digging for buried clues of a girlfriend, careful not to hit any like buttons, but it yielded nothing of interest. I'd learned from our conversation that evening that he was well-traveled, having been to thirty-six countries. He mentioned that he spoke Spanish and German. How cultured! And he didn't like sports. Weren't all men obsessed with sports? I had previously come to terms with the fact that whenever I dated or eventually married, I would have to put up with this flaw in their gender, yet, who would believe my luck? I'd found one who cared nothing for them!

A text asking me to dress up for a Friday evening date came three days later. I wasn't going to play it coy with this one. "I'd love to," I responded. I revisited the mall where this had all started, shopping for an outfit to lock down his interest. I left with six new options: a short red dress—too sexy? A pair of jeans with a silk top and stilettos—too casual? An African print dress—too cliché? I second-guessed every option; nothing was good enough. Obsessed, I FaceTimed my friends to show them all the outfits, summoning them to a vote. Alas, we went with a black knee-length dress that showed just a touch of cleavage.

Great conversation carried us through the date. An Italian restaurant nestled in Redwood City, with dim lights, candles on the tables, and a single rose in a tiny glass vase, nurtured us. We both turned down the drink menu, sipping on still water. He ordered a basil pesto pasta with chicken. I decided on polenta with short-rib and swiss chard. My meal reminded me of the quintessential Zimbabwean dish, sadza, muriwo nemavegi. We flirted, trying a bite of each other's food, and shared a slice of tiramisu for dessert. We talked until only the two of us were left in the restaurant. We could see the waiter's anxious looks beckoning us to leave so they could close for the night. Two more dates ensued, and, giddily, I became his girlfriend. A win for the black woman!

I'd decided, after a disastrous college dating life, that I would be celibate in my relationships until I was sure they were headed somewhere. Now that I had this gem of a man, I had to tread this ground lightly so he wouldn't fall out of love with me. I enjoyed his kisses and desired them. The relationship was new, promising, and he looked like a dream. I would have to find a way of dropping this missile without scaring him away. All evening, I watched his square jaw as he took bites of his dinner, telling me about his dreadful boss and lazy coworkers. I chewed my upper lip in anticipation of the conversation we'd have to have.

"You're quiet tonight? What's wrong? What's on your mind?" he asked, putting his utensils down, taking a sip of water, and reaching across the table for my hands.

I sighed, averting his eyes.

"You can tell me. What is it?"

I closed my eyes as tightly as I could and exhaled. "I'm not yet ready for sex in our relationship," I said, sounding much like Kylie with the frog in her throat.

He paused. I waited for a response. Nothing. I slowly opened my left eye. He laughed.

"What is that face?" I opened both my eyes, searching for his.

"Neither am I," he said, as he squeezed my hand. I stared at him, waiting for the laughter, the joke, but it never came. He picked up his utensils and continued eating.

The first time he stayed over wasn't planned. His car battery was flat one evening after work, so he took an Uber to my place. It was closer. He walked into the master bedroom I rented and sat on the king-sized bed. The landlady's house was riddled with cat hair, replete with antiques. We walked into the room and sat on the king-sized bed. I shooed away the orange cat following him. "I hate those things. I don't know why she needs so many. I bought my own bedding, though, and keep the door closed," I explained, distancing myself from the crazy, old cat lady.

"I don't mind cats," he responded as he lay on the bed, inviting me in for a cuddle.

We folded into each other's arms, and soon his lips found mine, and mine his, exposing what we felt inside. We slid under the covers as I felt his fingers caress my arms, then my stomach, then linger below my waist.

"No," I said with a smile, gently pulling his hand away. He smiled back and landed a firm kiss on my lips, and tried once more. "I said no," I repeated, wanting to sound as gentle as possible. Black women are known for being angry and for responding disproportionally to any triggering event. I didn't want to fit that stereotype. And I didn't want him thinking that I wasn't in love with him. After a few more no's, I stopped fighting and simply cringed. He laughed and carried on. It didn't proceed beyond him being handsy because of the celibacy vow, but I felt violated. I let him fall asleep beside me. All night I rehearsed what I'd say to him. I couldn't live through another night of discomfort.

"Good morning, beautiful," he said, beaming as he planted a wet kiss on my lips. He paused and caressed my fingers, tracing my nose and then lips with the edges of his fingers. "You're intoxicating." I smiled and took a deep breath. His voice grew soft, and so did the words I'd prepared all night.

"I see a forever with you," he said as he kissed me again, biting my lower lip. I shut my eyes. This wasn't the right time to talk. The trouble with renting a room is that there is nowhere else to go when you bring a guy over. By default, you lead him to your bed, skipping many steps and conversations that may have occurred had you invited him to your living room instead.

We went out for breakfast, and I drove him to the garage to pick up the mechanic, then took them both to his car. All afternoon I wrestled with myself. Since there was no penetration, and he was my boyfriend, and I did love him, and I had agreed to let him stay the night, even grabbing breakfast with him the morning after, did I have the right to feel violated? It had taken too long to find the otherwise perfect man. Was there ever a reason to bear more than you're comfortable with for the sake of a relationship? I was still finding my voice with him, perhaps still finding my voice with my-self. It's so much more complicated when you love him.

Two weeks passed, punctuated with soft forehead kisses, pic-nics at the beach, hiking trails, and late nights sharing dessert at rooftop bars. The man I'd been enamored with was back, stronger than ever, my previous disappointment in him fading, forgiveness blossoming. I let him spend the night again.

The cycle began anew, cuddles and kisses that led to hands in places where I didn't want them, no's that were ignored, mornings that started with a smile, a kiss on the cheek, and the "I love you's" as though I hadn't told him to stop. This time, I began ghosting him, ignored his calls, and ignored his texts for a few days. In silence, I heard my soul's anguish more clearly. I knew I needed to walk away. I requested to meet with him. At the very least, I could be decent and break up with him in person.

We met at a park by the bay in South San Francisco. A chilling front blew over the water, sending my fingers into hiding. Yellow spring wildflowers covered the shore amid the light green freshly budding grass. My plan was to take a walk. This way, I wouldn't have to look into his eyes when describing my discomfort. Cloud cover settled over us, selecting the prime position to hear my speech. The wind caused the water in the bay to cringe. It harassed me, frisking and groping us, imposing its unwanted company, sifting through our clothes, right to our flesh. We scurried to the car.

"This isn't working," I said.

He turned to me, teary-eyed. "Why are you breaking up with

me?" he choked. Without giving me a chance to answer, he launched into a soliloquy about what I meant to him and how he believed this was the relationship to last forever. I let my frustration flow, talked through just how uncomfortable he'd made me, and referenced our initial conversation about me not being ready to have sex. He listened, nodding, wiping his tears with his sweater. In a few minutes, he was full-on bawling, snorting and all. Murume mukuru, makambozviwonepi? – Really? I had fallen in love with him, allowed him to court my typically shy soul, and he hadn't gone all the way, so was I overreacting? With each tear that dropped, the hurt and spite that I'd gathered dissipated. What man cries over losing me? Within thirty minutes, he was out of tears, and I was out of spite. As our lips met passionately, I found myself surprised at how good it felt. I took him back.

He lived in San Carlos and rented a bedroom in a home where the landlord lived downstairs with his younger sister across the hall from him. Any time we were cuddling in his room, and he thought his sister might come in, he made me hide under the covers. I was a grown woman but felt like a teenager. "I want to set a good example for my sister," he'd say, or "I don't want my landlord to think ill of me because I let you spend the night." I'd smile and wonder, *so you're protective of your sister, who is almost my age and wouldn't want her doing what we are doing, but you aren't protective of me?* I wondered about my landlady as well. She didn't like him and made it well known, yet he continued to insist on spending the night at my place, away from the prying eyes of his landlord, to keep his reputation safe, caring not for what my landlord would think of me.

Whenever he spent the night, I was stuck in a nightmare. Kissing and cuddling that I very much wanted and enjoyed would often turn steamier than I desired. I said no, but I was ignored, and shame on me for letting it go. Early one evening, he forced my hands into his underwear and, with his hand over mine, massaged himself. What in my actions had led him to believe I wanted this? Perhaps

I led him on with my kisses. I swirled in confusion. It's one thing when he was reaching for me, but now that I had touched him, was I just as culpable?

We went out for a late dinner later that night. I was uncharacteristically quiet, studying the lines on the brown maple table. The fork and knife placement were inverted; I made the swap. A gray circle stained the corner of the table, probably from an unwelcome cup that sat there too long and leaked. An ailing candle sat at the center, swaying reluctantly, flickering like my love for him, candle wax melting away like my interest, settling at the base like my hurt. I looked at the stain, picked up my napkin, dipped it in my water glass, and wiped vigorously at it, wondering if it would ever come out, if the table would ever be new again, if my heart would ever be whole again.

"What's wrong?" he asked.

"Nothing," I responded in a whisper.

Was that lie confirmation that what had happened was okay? We'd talked about it so many times I was beginning to feel like a nuisance, a nag who says the same thing over and over again. Although he knew that I wouldn't budge on penetration, I was beginning to feel like I had already broken my vow.

Sensing my withdrawn heart, he reached across the table, adopted a serious tone, and brought up marriage.

I searched his eyes. His words sounded more like, "Will you just have sex with me already?" than "Will you marry me?" I told him I needed time.

It wasn't long until he began hounding me: *"You must make up your mind soon. I won't last very long. I won't wait around forever, you know."*

A month later, we were back at the same restaurant. I crumbled under the pressure and told him he could walk away. He changed his tune, told me he would wait for however long it took, that he had spoken carelessly, that I couldn't hold his words against him forever. "I was tired," he said. "This relationship or any other that you attempt will never work if you can't forgive—if you hold everything I say against me." Matakanaka ega – Nonsense. I stared at the stain on the table, knowing that whoever left the glass there probably didn't do it intentionally. Perhaps if they understood the result of their actions, they would make different choices next time. I took him back.

On a beautiful hike in the hills of Montara, overlooking the ocean, we started talking about our exes. He mentioned that his previous girlfriend was weird because she didn't know anything about sex; she let him do whatever he wanted with her body, but, through it all, she never moved. At that moment, I knew all too well what she had felt in those moments of being touched while frozen. I didn't need to hear more of the story to understand her pain, her confusion, her love for him, and his insistence. I knew he wasn't a womanizer by any means and was careful to a fault about leading women on. Perhaps that's why it was so hard for him to see the harm he was causing me, the last girl. Perhaps that's why I stayed so long. He was better than most men out there, right?

Later that evening, I lay next to him, feeling the coldness of his embrace. Being held but not permitted to finish my sentences. Ever-present but feeling like he cared not to be a student of what made my heart ache, or smile, or resent him, unless, of course, he agreed. Feeling his chest rise and fall, I listened to him lecture on decisions I ought to make, how I ought to think or feel, or see the world. I closed my eyes and let the loneliness of the relationship percolate. I imagined this dance, this feeling of emptiness clinging to me almost as tightly as he clung to me, until death did us part.

After I walked out of the relationship the final time, he told me that our indiscretions were my fault, too, that I was trying to play the victim. I don't know, was he right? I surely didn't kick and scream. Why did I utter gentle no's when I was screaming on the inside? Maybe it was a lack of self-esteem, my need to be liked, my need to not be stereotyped. What I do know, though, is that my "no" that first night and any other night that we were intimate meant just that, *no*. It didn't mean *convince me*, or *I'm not sure*, or *I'm just being a little shy*. What I proclaimed with my mouth was what I wanted him to hear, despite whatever other *signs* he believed I was giving him. In any case, I'm not sure how much of this blame I ought to take on. I'll let you be the judge.

Dear Aunt Vimbai

Budding

Harare, Zimbabwe
Beginning of Grade Seven

My breasts were coming out, and I was aghast. I did not want them. The race had begun. Who would rise faster, my dreams or them? My body was being invaded as if suffering from a chronic disfiguring ailment. I was desperate for a cure.

Rummaging through my wardrobe, I found an old black t-shirt. Using my teeth, I made an incision at the seam. With my sinewy fingers, I ripped out a long piece from the neck of the t-shirt to the seam on the bottom of the shirt, the part that would normally sit on my waist. After successfully tearing the piece out, I tied it around my chest, determined to keep the appearance of a flat chest. My breasts were the size of a small pear and hung on my scrawny frame; it was overwhelming. I wanted to look just like I did a year ago. Urgh, the piece I cut out was too short to go around my torso.

Defeated, I crumbled to the dark blue carpet and sobbed.

I didn't want to be a woman. I was a girl. I loved being a girl; I was feisty and sassy. I could take on anyone. All the boys in my class had nothing on me. I ran faster, climbed to higher tree branches, beat them at math and spelling, and could take any one of them on in a fistfight. I had never seen grown women take on men the way I did. It was as if they withered and died as they grew. I observed passivity, obedience, etiquette, and a need for approval from those around them. I was going to have to change everything. When out with friends, no longer would I be able to join the shirtless football team; no longer would I strip down to my underwear and jump in the pool with the boys. My breasts would mean I was different, as though a new identity was tattooed on me. We weren't equals but separate species. Although society had already acquainted me with all the necessary behavior modifications that would be essential for my survival as a woman, I had never felt the need to comply be-cause I was not one of them.

I knew I would invite ogling stares from boys on Harare's streets. Venencia had no peace walking me home from school when she picked me up. It was catcall after catcall. Men followed us home as if left to ourselves; we had nothing to converse about. As though we needed their company, their rescuing. I tell you, it was all her breasts. They told the men that she was a woman, ripe for harvest. That's why they had always bothered her and not me. I was prettier, that much was obvious, but my lack of breasts said I was just a girl, and so they paid greater attention to her.

"Nakai! What are you still doing? You are going to be late for school," I heard my mother's raised voice from the kitchen.

If my mother called me a second time, I knew it would mean trouble, so I rummaged through my wardrobe once more, finding a t-shirt to wear under my school uniform dress. I layered a wool-en jersey over the uniform. It had been hot all week, and I knew I would bake in the heat, but better the sweltering heat than peeking breasts. After looking in the mirror once more to ensure my out-fit was adequately concealed, I slouched my chest inward, folded my arms over my chest, and wiped the tears away. Taking a deep breath, I told the girl in the mirror to be brave.

My father's sister, Tete, burst into the room at my mother's in-struction to check on me. She was always nagging about me not do-ing my chores well enough. She and her husband were visiting for the week. Tete was a tall, brawny woman with smooth skin, dark like charcoal. It glistened in the sun and even in the dark, always doused in Vaseline. Tete wore her hair in an afro that stood at least five inches above her head, defying gravity. On this day, though, she wore a head wrap, a dhuku to cover her afro, and a colorful zambiya cloth, with vibrant rainbow colors convoluted into indecipherable shapes, was wrapped around her waist. Tete's body had begun to haunt me, as did my mother's and any other female I was related to. I looked to them for clues of what horrors my genes might har-bor. Tete had a bottom so large that it appeared to have a concealed pulley system facilitating its movement. As the left cheek was hoist-ed up, the right dropped violently, vibrating wildly as it fell back into place, just in time for the pulley to hoist it back up again as it switched roles with the left, a seamless pattern. Her breasts, though large, weren't boisterous hooligans. They did not point, announcing their presence to all who stood in front of her, unlike Venencia's. Hers seemed timid, perhaps tired; they slouched, facing the ground in respect. Either way, I preferred hers. Although large, they had manners. They were modest. I tried to remember what Aunt Vim-bai's looked like, but I was too young to check for such things when she left for the U.S. years ago.

"Morning, Mama. Morning," I said softly as I poured a cup of tea.

"Why are you wearing that woolen jersey in this heat?" my mother remarked. "Take it off."

My heart raced. "I *need* it," I said, clutching tightly onto it, ready for Mama to rip it off me.

"You want to faint in class? Heat exhaustion is no joke," she warned.

There she goes again, lecturing about health. Do this and you'll get sick; do that and you will not get sick. There was no way I was leaving the house without my shield. I looked at my Dad with pleading eyes. He always came to my aid. With his eyes, he told her to abjure, much to my relief. I could always count on him.

"You can't see me, my young wife?" Tete's husband mocked. I pretended not to hear him as I took a seat next to my father.

"Nakai, don't be rude. He's only teasing," Tete said.

"Morning," I said reluctantly, without looking at him.

"You are his muramu, you know, if something happened to me, you become his wife since I have no younger sisters," Tete said.

I rolled my eyes, but my face was hidden from everyone as I scooped a teaspoon of sugar into my tea. I looked at my chest and remembered not to take deep breaths.

The second born in my father's family, Tete was the only daughter out of seven children. I would become my uncle's inherited wife should my aunt die, at least, theoretically. In the meantime, while my aunt was alive, it was customary for uncles to flirt with nieces.

Tete's husband looked at me and tugged on my jersey. I shrugged his hand off in contempt.

"I don't want you for a wife anyway," he joked. "See how emotional, uptight, and inquisitive she is at such a young age? Kacha-tinetsa - I shudder to imagine what will become of her once she's fully grown. After all, women are notorious for being moody, unreasonable, and having no reign over how they feel," he mocked.

I ignored him, my ego battered from the punch of his words. I had quickly learned that voicing discomfort and questioning what he and other uncles said would promptly earn you a label. His remarks were much to the delight of my family; they laughed. To dignify myself and appear high-strung, I pretended his jokes did not bother me. Slowly, I began taking every emotion captive, careful to suffocate each one, at least in the presence of others; after all, I did not want to be considered a woman, much less a *typical* woman.

• • •

Dear Nakai,

I can't tell you how excited I get every time I receive a letter from you. I want to remind you that I'll always be here for you. No matter what's happening in your life, you can share candidly with me. Although I can't be in Zimbabwe to watch you grow, and I'm not sure when the next time I get to see you will be, rest assured, we'll go through all of life together, even through letters.

I laughed at your description of Tete's breasts. Remember this, though, women's bodies come in all manners of shape and form, and no matter the size or your shape, you are more than a vessel. It's been a journey for me, but I'm learning to love my body and find beauty in every season. This is only the start of what will be a lifelong journey, but I promise to always be by your side.

Love,

Aunt Vimbai

Before

Grade Four

"SLOW DOWN, WOMAN. I want to marry you."

Venencia looked to the ground and squeezed my hand tighter. Remaining silent, she picked up her pace. In the sweltering summer heat, our hands tautly clad around each other quickly became sweaty and sticky. The sun, blazing hot, was right above my eyebrow, smirking at and reveling in our misery. We grumbled yesterday about the heat, agreeing that it could not possibly get any hotter. I was convinced the sun heard the challenge and set out to prove us wrong. Even the flower petals and leaves bowed, begging for mercy in their droop.

"What's wrong? You can't talk?" he said blithely, putting his arm around her shoulder.

Venencia shrugged it off, still not saying a word.

"You're still young. I can tell these aren't your children. You're just another house girl, aren't you? Watching your madam's children? Your breasts are teeming with life, ripe and unperturbed," he laughed at her silence. "You would have to have been this one's age when you had your firstborn if they were yours," he said, pointing at me.

"Little one, how old are you?" he asked me.

"Nine," I responded.

"This isn't your mother, right?" he said, shifting his attention from me to Venencia.

I looked at Venencia; she gave me a stern and disapproving look. I knew not to answer. He pressed on, following us, nonchalant at the snub body language we reeked. He cared not for our reserve and blatant disdain for his company. The man declared undying love for Venencia, his intentions of marrying her, building her a home, and blessing her with his offspring to rear. He spoke passionately. I might have believed him, except he had just met her. It had been no more than five minutes since he first laid eyes on us. I wished he were an anomaly.

I grew accustomed to whistling as we walked; car windows rolled down. A whirlwind of shallow praises and insults hurled at us. Venencia was in a fishbowl, a prize to be won, prey to lust, subject to egos. I watched her get treated as though she was hollow, nothing more than a shell. She was a painting to be admired, critiqued, bought, and hung. A territory to be conquered, subdued, exploited, and discarded. I observed the compulsory game in which she must partake. Men ambushed her with abandon—she was caged with no circumvention. I witnessed her appraisal by appearance, and watched her valuation determined. I felt for Venencia.

The man pursuing us became agitated by our silence. "How ungrateful you are!" he said. "I did you a favor by noticing you in the first place. I approached you out of the kindness of my heart to help boost your self-esteem since the rest of the women walking up the street are far more attractive. What an uneducated fool. Ugly girl!"

His response was quintessential of men when they received a cold shoulder in response to their impassioned advances. It was appalling how quickly they flipped from confessing flaming designs for Venencia to vehemently affronting her with all manner of repugnant insults. It saddened me, yet for some reason, Venencia never seemed bothered. Either that, or she masked her true feelings in an attempt to cheer me up. She often told me not to worry, warning that engaging them was the surest way to guarantee they would never leave. Silence was our savior.

One suitor, however, was making an abiding impression on me. His name was Mateo. For all of last month, he had waited for us every day at the corner of Piers Road. If another man was already trying his luck with Venencia, he moved in and asked the suitor to stop bothering his wife. Meanwhile, Venencia still ignored him. He resorted to offering me candy, then asking benign questions about Venencia. I knew Venencia did not want me to tell Mateo anything about her, but I wanted the candy. I failed to get away with candy in exchange for no information of value in return. I learned from one of my classmates that the finest tactic is not to ignore them but to tell lies. Lie about everything. So, I told Mateo whatever fantasies my mind conjured up.

I initially told him that her name was Patience, and she was my sister. The problem was, I never could recall all the falsehoods I told Mateo. Over time, I could not keep my story straight. I often slipped and said her real name or said something terribly funny that made Venencia burst out in laughter. Mateo had figured out that if he stuck around long enough, he would get to know Venencia through me. Little by little, day by day, he gathered bits about our lives. I did not always mind. Truth be told, I liked the candy more.

He kept all the other men away.

Venecia began to fall for him, but I noticed how he stared at other women when they walked by. He couldn't have been genuine, yet she continued gushing about him because he said he wanted to marry her. I know Aunt Vimbai would never fall for this. The poor woman was a fool, the kind I hoped to never become.

• • •

Dear Nakai,

You define beauty.

I'm tired of the world's beauty standards. Fatigued by how physical attractiveness is the only thing the world talks about when it comes to women. It breaks my heart that you're already picking up on the objectification of women at such a tender age. It may take slightly varied forms in the U.S., but unfortunately, I have to deal with it as well. Don't buy into the lies that all that matters is the outside. We are so much more than our looks, and no one can assign or take away your worth. We can write our own narrative.

Love,

Aunt Vimbai

Brothers

Still Grade Four

IT HAD BEEN A while since our home had multiple visitors staying for an extended amount of time, but when my paternal grandfather died, the entire clan gathered at our home. The women cooked meals, and the men sat outside to talk. Hoping to escape chores, I sat with the men. Uncle Mandla, my mother's only brother, was with a few other relatives his age, most of whom I did not know. Some very well may have been funeral crashers, present just for the food and drinks. The men drank beer and exchanged stories. A tipsy Uncle Mandla recounted a story of how he discovered Faith, his girlfriend's younger, hotter sister. He described her ravishing beauty, boasting of how full her body was. A short man with a beard, perhaps another one of my distant uncles, asked him how he pulled off sisters.

"Rinonyenga rinohwarara, rinozosimudza musoro rawana – The animal that hunts crouches, keeping its head low, only reverting to its regular posture after the kill. Pretend to be the consummate gentleman, shower her with compliments, patiently listen, and lure her in. As soon as she commits and relinquishes her guard, let the fangs show, and never again treat her like you did in the early days. Women are brainless, utterly stupid, I tell you," Uncle Mandla scoffed.

Coming from a man I loved, these words were inscribed as the absolute truth in my mind. My heart was deflated.

At least I wasn't part of *that* tribe. I was just a girl, not a woman. I forcibly joined the men in their laughter.

• • •

Dear Nakai,

I haven't heard from you in a while. I hope all is well. I want to remind you that you're strong, beautiful, and walk in your own lane, and don't let anyone ever stifle your light.

I've included a few stamped return envelopes so you can always write back without needing to speak to your mom, as much as I love my sister.

Love,

Aunt Vimbai

Bleeding

End of Grade Seven

THE YEAR MY BREASTS started coming out was the start of the remainder of the unraveling, beginning with my mother's discovery.

"Nakai. Is that blood? Where's it coming from?" my mother asked. I had been careless, and now I was exposed. The toilet did not flush properly, leaving blood-stained toilet paper in the chamber. Once breasts came out, it was downhill from there.

"Did you hurt yourself?" Mama inquired further.

Silence. I felt the shame rise from within and saturate the room. Avoiding her eyes, I looked down at my crooked fingers, twiddling them.

"Answer me," she said. "Did that come from your underwear?"

Silence. She knew, another person but Aunt Vimbai, and I knew that I was indeed a *woman*. My skin crawled at the thought of words.

"Have you become mute?" she said, annoyed.

I nodded. Not to say I was mute but to answer her original question.

"When did this start?"

Again, I did not answer.

"I'm talking to you!"

Why was she so irritated?

I made a quick calculation and lied. If I told her I had been concealing this for a year, I'd be in greater trouble. Initially, I was rolling up toilet paper and fashioning a makeshift pad, but after telling Aunt Vimbai, I had a secret stash of pads. I made Aunt Vimbai swear to never tell a soul. She began slipping money into my letters, told me about the best positions to lie in if I was in pain, which medication to ask for at the store, and even wrote scripts on how to tell Mama, though I decided not to use them. I knew *everything* about being a woman.

"Today," I said, looking at my fingers to avoid her eyes.

"What are you using?"

"Toilet paper."

"Come with me," she said, walking to her bedroom.

She pulled at the gold-colored knob on the top drawer of the cedar dresser, opening it. Searching, she pulled out a bag of cotton wool and threw it to me. It landed on the bed next to me. She instructed me to pull out a handful of cotton, fold it into an imperfect ball, place it over my underwear, and wear that instead of the toilet paper. Aunt Vimbai had warned me that Mama would probably buy me cotton instead of pads, let alone tampons.

"What do you know about this?" Mama asked. I did not answer. "Nothing?" she continued.

I didn't mention Aunt Vimbai because I did not want her to ask me what else she had told me.

"Well, the only lesson you need to grasp is this—mess around with boys, and you *will* get pregnant."

I nodded, fidgeting with my fingers, avoiding eye contact. Mama needed not to worry. I was n*ever* getting a boyfriend, never getting married. I could see how those men were.

• • •

"RUFARO IS GOING TO pick up your gift from Tete. She works at the Johnson and Johnson plant," my father said casually.

"What is the package?" I asked.

"You'll see when it arrives," he said with that usual smirk he wore when teasing me.

Half an hour later, Rufaro walked into the living room with a plastic bag full of menstrual pads. No! Mama let me down. Again. She not only had told Dad my secret but Rufaro, too. They even sent him to pick up the pads! Most of all, Tete knew. Life was about to become unbearable! Who else did she tell my business? Rufaro handed me the plastic bag with a smug look on his face. I yanked the plastic bag from his hands and ran to my room. That night, I skipped dinner, pretending to fall asleep early. I could not bring myself to face anyone. For a year, I had nursed and doted upon my secret, and in less than a week, Mama outed me to the entire world. Each supply of pads would last me three months, at which time, Tete brought another, or worse still, sent her husband or a stranger with them. Her husband escalated his chiramu as soon as he found out about my blood.

I avoided him every chance I got until someone, usually my mother or Tete, scolded me for being rude. On occasion, Dad and

Rufaro picked the pads up. Garikai, my six-year-old younger brother, threw tantrums because he wanted me to share my gift bags with him. I was relieved when I turned thirteen; it was time to start Form One at boarding school after completing my primary school education. Once I moved away, my period would no longer be a family affair.

• • •

Dear Nakai,

Sounds like you finally told your mom. I'm so proud of you! I was so worried about you dealing with this without anyone on the ground. It's been so hard for me not to say anything, but I gave you my word and didn't want to break that trust. I feel so relieved. You must as well?
Love,
Aunt Vimbai

Boarding

Form One

TICK TOCK, TICK TOCK. We moved in perfect synchrony, like puppets controlled by string, devoid of will or opinion. Negative reinforcement was the order of the day—whips for the obstinate, songs of praise for the subservient. Ripped of individuality and identity assigned, we were robbed in likeness. Like beasts of burden, having no voice in what is served in the trough, when to be milked, when to be on the plow, tilling the land, or when to be locked up, so we were. As the sun set beyond the mountains each day, so did our hopes. We never looked forward to a new day. It held no surprises and yielded no hope; just like yesterday, it was pregnant with promises of sustained uniformity. We woke up *when the bell rang*, went to breakfast *when the bell rang*, attended class *when the bell rang*, and retired to bed *when the bell rang*.

• • •

"NAKAI, GET UP. WE will be late for the run," Fari whispered. Pulling the blankets over my face, I ignored her, not wanting to get up.

"The matron is already taking roll outside the dormitory. She will begin inspections soon," she said, shaking me. The only things I appreciated about boarding school were the absence of Uncle Mandla, Tete's husband, and my father's rumbling snore. I had been on punishment all last weekend after accumulating four infractions over the week. One because my skirt was not at least four inches below my knee, one for whispering after lights out, another for being a few minutes late to dinner, and one more for a wrinkled shirt. Plus, my tie wasn't properly in place.

I was lucky Fari did not rat me out when she got caught whispering during the compulsory two-hour nightly study time. The teacher on duty had been patrolling classrooms with a whip in hand, ready to administer corporal punishment to noisemakers, or rather, whisperers. Fari and Chipo received three whips each when they were caught. Thankfully, they did not tell the teacher I was part of the conversation. I spent the weekend plucking feathers from slaughtered chickens for the school's Sunday lunch, weeding the garden, and incinerating used menstrual pads for my other infractions. However, I was still thankful to have escaped getting a beating, or worse yet, toilet scrubbing. I was always on the punishment list, no matter how obedient I was. For a while, I was sure the matron had it out for me. It appeared she had some unspoken bell curve for every rule. What was an acceptably clean uniform this week could land me on the punishment list next week. You would think Tete invented this school and paid the matron to keep me in line.

"I don't know how you go to class without taking a shower after these runs," Fari said once we made it outside. I shrugged my shoulders and kept running.

"The dry bath is enough. I don't know how you stand naked in that roofless showering gallery, pouring freezing water over your body in the midst of sheets of the morning fog," I replied. Fari shook her head. She was the only one who knew my secret. If the matron ever found out that I simply doused my towel in water and wiped down all the essential corners of my body from my room, punishment would be assured. Though I despised the freezing water at dawn, what I was truly avoiding at the assigned bath time was undressing in front of six hundred girls. The gallery was a large open room without privacy partitions. Each girl fetched water in a pail from a tap outside, carried it inside the gallery with a bar of soap in another, and washed it from the pail, seemingly oblivious of the hundreds of eyes that surrounded it. I cared nothing for showing the embarrassment my budding body proclaimed. These girls were a strange species, unbothered by femininity. I much preferred taking my bath at night, just before lights out when no one was watching.

I never told Fari the real reason why I did not like showering in the morning. She would not understand. Fari had told me she *wanted* breasts ever since she was a little girl. She even tried to fake having her period so that she could wear her older sister's menstrual pads in grade two. This perturbed me. She had been brought up in a female household, living with her parents, two aunts, and four older sisters. They openly talked about all the pleasant and not-so-pleasant changes that happen to female bodies. Fari understood adolescence would turn her into a woman early on and looked forward to it with alacrity. I feared she would judge me, even though she often went out of her way to assist me. Like most of these girls, Fari was incredibly kind, generous, and loving. All my uncles said it would be impossible to live cordially with six hundred girls. They said they would be catty and moody. Did we argue and tease each other at times? Yes, but no more than I did with my brothers back home. In fact, at times, the girls were a lot less dramatic than Rufaro or Tete's husband.

As the rest of the school headed to the gallery to bathe after the run, I remained in the dormitory, snacking on the jam I stored in an old lotion container. I got tired of the plain cornmeal porridge served in the dining hall. Since we weren't permitted to bring in any tuck from home, I smuggled food in. We are only allowed to bring toiletries, so I would empty some of my lotion containers, clean them out, and fill them with jam. I hid cereal in boxes of *Surf*—the laundry powder. I squeezed powdered milk for my cereal into empty toothpaste tubes and a packet of roasted nuts and chips in my menstrual pads package. This way, neither the prefects nor the matron suspected anything during the inspection of our storage trunks at the beginning of the school term. In fact, on the first day of school, I tied cool drink packets on a string, then tied the string around my waist and put a chocolate bar in each shoe. They were too busy searching the trunks, so it would never occur to them to search my body. I was always quick to hide the jam before my roommates returned from the gallery, getting a head start on my assigned daily morning chores, picking up litter around the classrooms before the matron inspected our work yet again for an opportunity to add to her weekend punishment list.

Becoming

Still Form One

I COULDN'T STAND THE girls at school. We were permitted to either watch a movie or go to the school hall to listen to music for two hours each week during the weekend. The films were too sappy for my taste, anyway. Some of these girls cried as they watched romantic movies. How pathetic! I was much better than them. Part of me believed they weren't always crying over the movie. I believed they were, in reality, lamenting over how burdensome life was in boarding school, but since complaining about teachers or the establishment was forbidden, the only outlet to let out all these emotions was by crying over movies. Around Valentine's Day, the music hall reeked with equally insufferable mawkish sentimentalism. I knew better than to waste time agonizing over any man.

"I can't stand the endless encore of Celine Dion and Westlife love songs. I'm not like the rest of you," I said as the sound of love-sick giggles wreaked from the entertainment room and echoed on the walls.

"Why do you always feel a strong need to separate yourself from the rest of the girls? To prove that you, unlike us, can't be tickled by love? Everything with you, Nakai, has to be a competition. Is this self-loathing? Does bringing the other girls down make you feel superior? We are *all* different, *all* unique, and this thing of trying to lump all women as one stereotype and yourself as the alpha lioness is pathetic," she snapped, hands on her hips before turning her back on me.

With that conversation, Fari revealed wounds I had no prior knowledge of. She was right—every girl in school *was* unique. Perhaps I just had never intimately known a large enough sample size of women, so I assumed they were all alike. I started to toy with the idea that perhaps not all Shona women grew up to live miserable lives. I began to realize that these girls *were* smart and dreamed of making an impact on those in their sphere. They wanted to have fulfilled careers to help make the world a better place. They also talked about being great moms to their kids someday.

"Why does choosing one mean giving up the other?" Chipo often asked when I made fun of her dreams of bearing children while I emphasized building a career. Some girls wanted to build orphanages and adopt an abounding number of children, never having any of their own biological offspring. Some wanted to be president; others wanted to be stay-at-home moms. Every dream was valid, and no girl was lesser because of her preferences. Around these girls, I was slowly growing somewhat comfortable with the idea of becoming a woman someday. I saw incredibly patient, loving, and kind souls who fully embraced their femininity. What I previously perceived to be female flaws now look like strengths.

Gradually, I found myself thinking, "Maybe this wasn't so bad. Perhaps I *could* be a woman and still be unique and different." Being a woman did not have to mean giving my identity up and assuming one assigned to me by society. Perhaps being part of this tribe *was* something I could be proud of. I could still make my own decisions while also disagreeing with their actions on some issues. I could be wildly varied and unique from every woman in the tribe, but their views did not have to be wrong in order for me to feel validated. I stopped fighting so hard to be excluded from them. I was learning that it was ok to be female, a proud woman, unique in my own way, but a woman all the same. Fari's reprimand was hard to accept yet altogether liberating. I felt like a miserable human.

• • •

Dear Nakai,

Women are unique. Growing up in our patriarchal society made me despise the idea of being a woman. When I was your age, being a woman was synonymous with oppression, having fewer opportunities, and being taken advantage of.

Instead of standing up as an example to show the world that women are capable, instead of being living proof that the stereotypes the world perpetuates about women aren't true, I, too, chose merely to separate myself. I recently resolved never to judge or describe any woman as inferior simply for views that differ from mine. I embrace every woman's uniqueness. No longer will I be flattered by statements such as, "Women are so.... (insert any derogatory remark), but you're different." I'll stand with my tribe.

I wish I could say that I'm completely beyond this struggle. Trust that when I'm writing to you, I am in part speaking to myself as well. I hope to be present to help you process so you never have to live through the self-loathing complex I endured. I hope you can be unapologetically female from a young age.

I truly yearn for the day when more women can shed the skin society forced us to don, being bold and unapologetically unconstrained once more.

Love,

Aunt Vimbai

Boys

Form Two

TENDAI STOOD LIKE A tower above the rest of the boys. He had beautiful, ebony smooth skin and large brown eyes. When he looked at you, his piercing gaze stared straight into your soul—undressing your inner parts, leaving you naked and exposed. His eyes unearthed fissures and crevices where you hid your most vulnerable self, whose very existence was unbeknownst even to you, at least until he peeled you open. I forbid myself from looking into them. I could not allow myself to be hypnotized. His lips were generous—his lower lip was especially full and luscious. He looked chic every time I saw him. He was the type to look at himself in the mirror protractedly before feeling dapper enough for the day. Tendai was the kind of guy you just knew had to be cocky, the kind of guy that, upon his entrance into the room, all the girls sat up straight and perked up their chests, hoping that he noticed them. It never happened, though. Tendai was not impressed.

The first time I saw him, I was startled by his ravishing looks. This took me aback. A boy's looks never arrested me. I was critical of any male, guarded, and never easily impressed. I was resolute to never let a man near me again. However, I was regularly tempted to be friendly and flirt even, but just as they began to think I was falling in love, I would turn around and break their sorry hearts before they could break mine. After all, I was certain that anything they could do, I could do better. If guys were out to get girls, perhaps I ought to beat them at their own game.

I was walking from Sam Levi's village during the December school holiday, my hair in long braids and tied in a ponytail, extended all the way down to my lower back. I always wore my hair in long, braided extensions during the school holiday. My pair of jeans, one size too big, loosely hung around my waist while a light blue spaghetti top exposed my perfectly sculpted arms. Tendai was bouncing a basketball on the street. He wore knee-high gym shorts and a light blue t-shirt. Our colors matched. I smiled to myself. His friend Kuda was with him. They dribbled the ball past each other with increasing resoluteness as I approached. I knew Kuda because our parents went to the same church. The large, triangle-shaped, brick building with white angels the size of Busta, our dog, guarded either side of the entrance. Angels were always white. I wasn't sure angels with skin like mine existed. Kuda was known as the troublemaker in the neighborhood. I overheard his mother talking to Mama once about sending him to the village where he would not have the luxuries of suburbia; perhaps hardship would teach him to behave. Although Kuda and Tendai were both my age—we had just turned fourteen—Kuda was already a womanizer. When he was sent to the village, the rumor was that he impregnated a much older woman there. His mother had recently brought him back to Borrowdale because here, she could at least keep an eye on him, and give him a curfew. Kuda once tried to befriend me, but I refused to reciprocate, guarded as I was. Whatever his narrative, I stayed far away.

I figured Tendai had to be similarly rogue. Men are all the same. I was certain Tendai was worse than Kuda because he was handsome. I did everything in my power to scare away all the boys who were previously my friends when we were younger. I was starting to recognize contrast in the way they whispered to each other as I crossed the road. They were looking at me differently. They commented on my hair and clothes and tried to be smooth around me. No, I wasn't the same girl they climbed trees with or raced down the street shirtless with. I was a mysterious, esoteric creature, mesmerizing. We weren't friends anymore. I was a romantic prospect.

I knew, however, that some of this interest was not a natural phenomenon that came with age. I recall running into Godhi, my childhood best friend, as he was walking with a few older boys, likely his cousins, who were visiting over the school holiday. After greeting them and parting ways, I overheard his cousins chide him about failing to make a move on a viable prospect. I continued walking, pretending not to hear what they said.

Godhi is like my brother! He could never look at me that way. They have no idea how far back we go, I sneered in my head.

Much to my chagrin, I was wrong. Godhi changed, and he clearly had designs toward me. Once, he even made a sorry attempt at a kiss, making our relationship painfully awkward. That was when I resolved to keep my distance from him and all the other boys in the neighborhood. The goal was to discourage any potential interest in me, but I soon realized I was achieving the exact opposite effect. My rare appearances on the streets made me unattainable. The culture loved a good chase—the more elusive and detached a female was, the more exhilarating the pursuit became, particularly when she continued to decline advances of *all* men.

Tendai, though, was different from the other boys in the neighborhood in that there was no history to complicate things between us. I did not grow up with him and hence, had no recollection of him wetting his pants because he was scared or falling off a tree and running home crying to his mother, as I did with most of the other boys in the neighborhood. He was veiled, mysterious. I was intrigued, but I knew I wasn't the only girl who was taking an interest. This greatly irked my personal mission to prove that I was unique. I was angry at myself for caring. Try as hard as I did to forget him, I found myself fantasizing and daydreaming about him.

Was he smart? Did he have a girlfriend? Of course he did. What was she like? What did he think of me? Did he like my braids? Were they too long? Did he have more than one girlfriend? Besides basketball, what else was he into?

• • •

GARIKAI SPRAWLED INTO THE house with two of his eight-year-old friends. He was roiled, rambling on and on about how "the boys" kept asking him about me.

"I just want to play cops and robbers. I don't want to spend the afternoon talking about my annoying sister," he said, throwing his hands in the air.

I knew I had a reputation for being formidable. I was fine with that. I cared nothing for these boys anyway. I rolled my eyes at Garikai's words until he said, "...especially Tendai..." whilst I sprung from the kitchen table.

"Garikai, did you say something about Tendai? Was he asking about me?"

"Yes."

"Are you sure it was him, not Kuda? He is usually with Kuda. Kuda is the yellow bone, the light-skinned one. Tendai is the tall, dark one." I cross-examined him, though, crossing my fingers that he was not mistaken.

"I know their names. Kuda told him not to bother trying because you don't hang out with any of them anymore."

"Well, what exactly did Tendai ask?" I inquired, launching my interrogation.

"He asked if I was your little brother and asked me to tell him what kind of things you like."

With that, Garikai scampered off to the living room; his favorite MaPopeye, Conan the Adventurer, was about to start, and I was being a bother.

I scurried after him. I needed more details.

"So, what did you say when he asked what I like?"

"Leave me alone! I don't remember," he whined as he set himself on Dad's sofa spot.

This was the most opportune sofa to sit on for TV watching as it directly faced it, unlike the others arranged in an arc around the TV. Dad's spot sagged low after years of everyone fighting to sit on it whenever he was not home.

"No, you need to remember!" I said, sounding more desperate than I anticipated.

"I just want to watch Conan the Adventurer. Get out of the way!"

I knew I would not win against MaPopeye. I resorted to bribing. "If you can remember what you told him, I will buy you chocolate."

His eyes darted back and forth, doing arithmetic in his head. Releasing an exasperated sigh, he scratched his head and shook his head—no, he'd pass on the chocolate.

If candy wasn't going to work, I knew what would. Busta, our dog, his soft spot.

He referred to Busta as his best friend. I knew that promising Garikai not only chocolate but my meat from dinner for Busta meant he would tell me everything I needed to know.

"I told him you like listening to music, and you dance when songs you like come on the radio, and I also told him that yesterday you fell down the stairs trying to dance and landed on your bum," he giggled, hysterically.

My eyes grew large, popping out of my head.

"That's it? What about how smart I am, or well-read, or accomplished I am at sports? None of that? You had to tell him about how I fell?" I let out an exasperated grunt and stormed out of the room.

"What about my chocolate?" he pouted.

"You don't get chocolate for that! Say something smarter next time," I yelled, annoyed, walking out. Now Tendai was going to think I was a clumsy clown. But why did I care so much?

I went to bed fantasizing about Tendai. If he was asking about me, he *must* be interested. I wondered what I would do if he asked me to be his girlfriend.

The truth was, I did not want to be his girlfriend. The idea of being a girlfriend was synonymous with a credulous, naïve vulnerability—gullibility that pries one to needless hurt and betrayal. I was simply intoxicated by the probability that he was fond of me. To what end, though, I wasn't sure. A significant part of me desired to know more about him. I was drawn to him in a way I had never been drawn to anyone before. I knew I had to gallantly guard myself – he was not to be trusted; no men were to be trusted. Now, don't get me wrong, I was fully aware that, at this age, I was dealing with a boy, not quite a man, but you know the ancient proverb: Mwana wenyoka inyoka – A baby snake is still a snake. Tendai created a paradox. Excitement and dread, anxiety and serenity, longing and disdain, all cohabiting within me, vacillating from one to the other like a pendulum. What was I guarding myself against? He hadn't even said he liked me, and I had only ever laid eyes on him a few times. Even on those few occasions, he barely said a word to me as Kuda did most of the talking. Perhaps, he was simply digging information for Kuda or some other friend of his.

The next few days were a game of sorts. Every time I heard the sound of a basketball bouncing out on the street, I quickly dressed up and took a walk in the street. I pretended to be going for a stroll or to see a friend, but I wanted to run into him. I fixed my hair and cycled through five or more outfits before being satisfied that I had picked one he might like. When we saw each other, he greeted me and briefly asked how I was doing—never more, never less. Whenever he stretched out a hand in greeting, the warmth of his body sent tingles down my back. I held onto his hand for two seconds longer than I otherwise would any other handshake. My heart fluttered. He looked at his shoes most of the time we spoke, which told me he wasn't interested. I did not mind much when he looked down, though. It put me at ease because it meant I did not have to worry about his giant, piercing eyes silently probing me. I wondered about the warmth of his lips, given what his hands exuded. I looked forward to seeing him. Each encounter gave an exhilarating rush, albeit brief and fleeting. It wasn't long until debasement filled me, disgusted that I was curious about a kiss.

• • •

Dear Nakai,

You like a boy! I'm so excited for this phase of your life. Oh, it'll be so much fun to share stories. I'll tell you more about the first boy I ever had a crush on in subsequent letters.

Love,

Aunt Vimbai

Buffoons

Still Form Two

"NAKAI! I TOLD HIM I had a message for him. I told him what you wanted me to say. Can I get my chocolate now?" Garikai said, jumping up and down with excitement.

"Told whom, what?" I asked. I knew exactly what he meant. The pit in my stomach overturned. Never had I been so terrified about the words my younger brother may utter.

"I saw him and told him that you were mad at me for telling him that you fell on your bum. I also told him that you said you would get me chocolate if I told him about how smart and accomplished you are, and how you can play basketball and beat him and that you like to read," Garikai bragged, hands outstretched, expectant for his well-earned reward.

"You did what?!" I screamed. I was ruined. Now he knew I had a crush on him. He wasn't supposed to know. Garikai outed me! I had let myself down. I was ordinary, no different from all those other girls who published their crush on him abroad. Worse still, Garikai told him I bribed a child with chocolate in exchange for feeding him information about me. This was *not* what I meant when I told him to say something smarter next time. There goes my reputation. My greatest fear was realized: I was just your average girl.

"What did he say?" I inquired, my eyes tightly shut, not sure I wanted to know.

"He did not believe me. He asked if you would say yes if he asked you to play basketball with him." My fear turned to excitement in an instant, a transition that I had become all too familiar with lately.

"And..."

"I said you are good at the game, plus that you come first at everything in school, so he might lose."

"Good boy! What did he say?" I said, hugging him and listening more intently than ever.

"I don't remember. I want to watch Popeyes now." He switched on the TV, banging it on its silver top three times. The gray, white, and black dots on the screen twinkled, and by the third bang, brighter colors appeared. Garikai stared at it as though to warn it of another impending beating if it did not behave. At his unspoken countdown, mangled characters appeared, and soon, the picture was back in focus. Echoes of moving purple and red light from the characters on the screen tinted the room.

Typically, I would press harder but refrained, drawing lessons from the previous encounter. Instead, I lay on the sofa and daydreamed about Tendai asking me to play basketball. Would I truly play, or would I be soft and let him win? If I play well, he may feel dominated by a girl and stop liking me. I heard from Venencia that boys are more drawn to girls whom they feel superior to.

"*It helps their egos,*" she said.

My head swirled with questions. So, what if he liked me? Then what? We date? What if he cheated? What if he tried to touch me beyond a kiss? I could not have anyone touching me. Why did I even like him? What was the point of all of this? It's not like we were going to get married. We were too young; besides, I wanted to be someone important and have my own money before I got married. I was determined to never end up like one of these house girls. Marriage? The word tasted like gravel in my mouth. Did I say 'marriage'? Why was I even thinking about marriage? I did not want to ever get married! It *would* certainly be precious if he chose me, though. All the other girls would be jealous. I wondered if he was nice. I knew for a fact that he did not harass girls in the street, which was a good first step. Perhaps he was one of the good ones. He must be, right?

I could hardly sleep when night fell. My designs toward Tendai percolated every thought like an unwanted visitor overstaying his welcome. I eschewed dinner. I had no appetite, ambushed by sentiment. I sure hoped he was kind.

The next time I heard a basketball bouncing, I got ready and walked out to the street, hoping to run into him. I was sure he bounced his basketball right in front of our gate, so I knew that he was there—a secret call. He stayed there, dribbling alone until I came out. This time was different. This time, he dared to ask a second question.

"Your brother tells me that you play basketball, too. Is that true?"

"A little," I responded, feigning modesty.

"How come you have never said anything?"

"How come you have never asked?"

"I did not want to assume you have the same interests as me. Besides, you always look so proper and well put together in your dresses and long braids. You don't seem like the sporty type."

"Wearing a dress and having my hair done doesn't mean that I'm not athletic," I protested.

"You're right. I'm sorry," he said.

Oh no! I was scaring him away. I was being too sassy. He stopped talking and remained quiet. Should I say something? Had we been quiet for too long? Silence. Still silence. What would I say? What if

I sounded stupid?

"Dresses are all my mother buys me nowadays," I added.

He did not respond. My heart was in my stomach again. My knees buckled. Was I crumbling? Right in front of him? What happened to the confident girl?

Get yourself together, Nakai! Are my hands shaking? He is going to know. Quick! Hide them behind your back. Wait. Are his hands shaking? He likes me! He likes me!

I slowly convinced my nerves to simmer down. As I slipped out of them as one removes a dress, my confidence steadily returned. I smiled, wide and bright, exposing my perfectly white, chiseled teeth. I knew I was smiling widely but could not help myself. There was something endearing about his timid manner. I must mean *something* to him. A minute passed, but we remained silent, both of us carefully curating our thoughts, playing out all the potential outcomes of a conversation yet to be uttered. We calculated and revised each word cautiously before daring to allow any to escape our lips. Finally, he spoke.

"Um, is there any chance you would be willing to play with me sometime?"

I was amused because he asked. Men usually insisted that you join them. And if you weren't interested, they berated you and explained how they were doing you a favor by offering their company. Yet here was Tendai, exuding such humility and gentleness. His demeanor told me that *I* would be doing *him* a favor by saying yes.

I did not want to seem easy. I had heard that was not a good thing. Was I supposed to play hard to get? He seemed like he was the type to respect my *no* and thus, cease his pursuit. I was confused.

"If you would rather do something else like watch a movie or come swimming at my place, I can do that, too," his voice cracked. His fledgling pubescent baritone voice flailed, sounding like a six-year-old girl. I realized I had been so lost in my thoughts that I had neglected to speak. I hadn't responded to his offer to play basketball. He was reaching, desperately so. He was willing to do whatever I wished, just to spend time with me. I was smitten. It wasn't just those big brown eyes anymore. He had a heart of flesh. He cared. He liked me!

We settled on swimming at his parent's house the next afternoon. I was so giddy that I barely slept or touched my food. My stomach was already content, chock-full of my heart. Usually, the one dominating conversation at the dinner table, I sat quietly, aloof. My father remarked that I seemed absent, but I contrived some excuse about eating a late lunch and being antsy due to my impending return to boarding school. It sufficed; no one pressed further. I wished there was someone I could tell. I had never cared for a sister, but I desperately wanted one at this moment. Better yet, I wished Aunt Vimbai was here; she would know what to do. After helping Venencia with the dishes, as was expected of me, I joined the living room where Rufaro and Uncle Mandla sat, listening to their conversation.

"I met a man today. It's only the smooth, beardless face that told me that perhaps I was speaking to a woman. This woman's body looked just like mine. Nothing to touch on the chest and a behind as flat as a man's," Uncle Mandla laughed churlishly as he scratched the scar on his neck.

"What man is attracted to his own body? She had nothing to look at. I tell you. These are the kinds of women who become tsikombi – unmarried in their old age. She can never satisfy any man."

Rufaro laughed, "God help her. That's a hard curse to live under."

I lowered my eyes toward my chest, ruminating on what he said. He was right. I'd seen it all my life: attractive women were large and curvy. Here I was, planning to go swimming with Tendai tomorrow. My one-piece bathing suit would bare my body in broad daylight in a manner Tendai had never quite witnessed before. He would know that I was not a woman. I was scrawny, my bum was flat, and my breasts small. Were they too small? How could Tendai be attracted to me? Would *I* become a tsikombi? For the first time, I spired for larger breasts, though not quite for breasts, rather for attention—Tendai's affection. Yet still, not so much attention but validation, reassurance that I was whole, enough, beautiful, desirable, *worthy*. Surely I could not enchant any sane male in my current form. The realization nourished my insecurities, torturing me. My joy at the prospect of our date turned into apprehension, apprehension into despair, and despair into self-loathing. I wasn't good enough. I would never be enough without the ideal body, whatever *they* decided that was.

● ● ●

Dear Nakai

I'm dying to know what happened with Tendai. You can't leave me hanging like that!

Love,

Aunt Vimbai

Buckling

I CUPPED MY BREASTS in the mirror. They did not seem to have grown much at all over the last few years. A fresh prayer rose within me. Hesitating, I slowly went down on my knees. "God, I want to be beautiful. Please give me breasts so Tendai can see my beauty. I promise this is the last time I pray about my breasts. Don't make them too big, though. I don't want them to look like those women who seem to have a second butt on their chest. Just chase away all the other men who might become attracted to me as a result. I just need this one person to like me. Amen." Anxiety settled in the crevices of my mind. I cuddled myself on my bedroom floor, and there, I fell asleep.

I woke with clarity about one thing, though: I was not going swimming. Why had I picked *that* out of all possible activities? I would have been better off playing basketball. At least that way, he would not get a candid look at my shapeless body. Hesitating, I found a few socks, rolled them into balls, and stuffed them in my shirt to give the illusion of a slightly bigger bust. The socks rolled straight down, out of the shirt, and onto the blue carpet. I did not own a bra. Mama never bought me one. I never wanted one either. A bra would have meant acknowledging that my body was changing, and before now, I wasn't ready for it.

As morning settled in, I watched the brown, wooden clock that hung on the living room wall above the TV. Its black hands ticked at a pace much slower than I'd ever observed, loudly counting the seconds to my embarrassment. With each cycle, they wound up anxiety as the slowest of the three hands steadily crept to the number two—the time we agreed to meet. I watched a housefly zoom to the TV, then to the clock, rest on a window, dance in my face, crawl on my leg, and when I tried to smack it, it zoomed to the TV, then repeat. All morning long, it heckled me. Two o'clock struck and passed with me huddled on the sofa, still watching the hands cycle, still watching the fly. The sound of the basketball bouncing outside got louder about an hour after our date was due. I locked myself in my room, eluding him. Garikai, the eager messenger, knocked on my door, and I sent word that I had taken ill and would not be available.

• • •

IT HAD BEEN A week. I was walking home from Sam's Village to run Mama's errands. Pay the electricity bill, then the water bill, buy two loaves of bread, and three kilograms of beef. "Nakai!" he called out from behind me. My intestines tied themselves into half-stitch knots. Without turning my head, I increased my pace. My parent's gate was only a few more yards away. If I was fast enough, I could make it there before having to face him. He ran until he caught up with me. This time, he wore a confidence too large for him. I had grown accustomed to him as a coy boy, yet he had a resoluteness about him. He must've replayed this scene recurrently. He did not search for words as he usually did. Rather, they flowed swiftly, as though rehearsed and leaving his lips for the thousandth time.

"Nakai, I'm sorry if I did something wrong. I just wanted to spend time with you. I like you and would like to get to know—" he began.

"I'm not interested in swimming with you," I snapped, as though he was responsible for my flat chest.

"I assumed you wanted to swim. You chose that out of all the other options. What do you like to do? I'll spend time with you in whatever way you like."

I exhaled deeply.

"You know, we don't even need to do anything. We can just talk. You are just so different."

I rolled my eyes despite the caress of his words. I had heard that line before. "Let me guess. I'm the most ravishing being your eyes have ever beheld?" I chuckled.

He began to speak but paused. His hands were in his pockets, fidgeting while his left foot tapped nervously on the concrete slab, begging the earth beneath his feet to awaken and speak, to spew out wisdom and direction on how to respond. He must not have rehearsed for this part. His confidence slithered to his feet, exposing a frightful fourteen-year-old boy. I turned my back to him and walked away, my heart like a pendulum swinging from intoxication. He *is* fond of me, to abasement, he is *never* going to speak to me again, to repletion, I'm *not* easily fooled like other girls, and back to intoxication, he *is* enamored.

It felt like I was hanging onto a tree that was being swept up in a tornado, invincible gusts sweeping through and decimating everything I thought I knew. I did not trust boys. I was so sure that I would never desire their attention. Wasn't every male like Uncle Mandla, deception incarnate? If Tendai wasn't the same yet, it was just a matter of time until he came of age, grew fangs, and produced venom. I was better than this, yet here I was, crying out to God for bigger breasts so that Tendai could notice me. Who was I? Something was restive within me. A boisterous, crass girl was chained deep inside, kicking and shrieking in rebellion. I heard her thuds in my blood, right above my left eye. She fought for emancipation, desiring to fall for a boy. She could die for all I cared. That meddlesome girl would never see the light of day. I hoped she would suffocate. I had no room for foolery, none for weakness. Love was not welcome.

I walked away from Tendai and begrudgingly joined Uncle Mandla, Venencia, and Rufaro for lunch in the living room. At least they kept me grounded on the realities of the world, preventing me from being swept up in a sea of teenage emotions. Uncle Mandla was a faithful reminder that Tendai was a man in the making. About thirty minutes or so after joining them, the living room phone rang, and Garikai called my name.

"A boy is on the phone asking for you."

All eyes turned to me. Rufaro, Uncle Mandla, Sisi Venencia. Their eyes flooded with disapproval and condescension. From the disappointment on their faces, you would think they found me riding a hyena—an activity reserved only for witches. Garikai, the only one who knew I had been fraternizing with a boy, announced to everyone, "It's Tendai!"

I picked up the rotary phone, carefully moving the cord around the padlock that sat between the zero and one dialing key, restricting the ability to turn the dial. The padlock was in place to prevent us from potentially running up the bill. We could only receive calls with the lock but not make any, at least not with the dial. We found a workaround, though, tap dialing. When dialing a number, we simply tapped the switch hook the corresponding number of times for each digit to make an outgoing call.

With four pairs of eyes on me, observing in palpable silence, I told Tendai that I could not come out to swim with him anymore or spend time with him in any other way. Dejected, he asked if he could do anything to change my mind. I told him my mind was made up and hung up. Lifting my head, I met Rufaro's disgusted stare. Perhaps more horrified than disgusted.

"You are now getting involved with boys, huh?" he sneered.

"Swimming? Showing off your body, too? You know guys just want one thing, right?"

Venencia laughed, "Leave her alone. What body? Those mosquito bites on her chest don't count as a woman's body. They are just kids playing. It's all innocent," she remarked.

My heart sank. I stared at my chest.

• • •

THERE WAS NO WAY I was ever dating Tendai. No way was I ever going to be among the stupid. This is why I never wanted to become a woman, to begin with. I'd already seen it all. I knew how all this ended, and I wasn't interested. I rushed to my room and picked up my journal. I just wanted it all to go away.

Dear Aunt Vimbai...

The Zimbabwean Dream

Rudo stepped out of the cold room, hiding her phone under her apron. Feeling her heartbeat in her ears, she looked around to make sure no one was in sight. Messages had been buzzing all morning, and now her cousin was calling. She felt her legs disappear beneath her. Drops of sweat formed around her hairline, dampening the hairnet that clung tightly to her forehead. This was risky, but she had to answer the phone.

"Mbuya has foam coming out of her mouth. She is having fits, and at times, her body becomes stiff, throwing her in unbearable pain," Tinashe exclaimed, her anxiety palpable.

Mbuya, Rudo's maternal grandmother, had raised her after her father received a job at the mine and her parents had to move to a town with no school. Now she was living in Dallas and hadn't seen her grandmother in twelve years. Mbuya was on her death bed, and she would not get to say goodbye.

"We would take her to the hospital if we had the money. The doctors in the public hospitals are on strike, and the private hospitals are charging in US Dollars. Mbuya will need some expensive medication, maybe an operation. You know how all the medication is imported from South Africa nowadays. We are looking at almost four thousand dollars," Tinashe told her, choking on his words, overwhelmed by grief.

Rudo winced at the cost. That headache that felt like a noose tied around her head emerged. That was twice her gross monthly income, earned by working at the meat plant, driving for Uber on weekends, babysitting for neighbors, and, occasionally, braiding hair.

"Don't worry about it. I will find a way to send you the money," Rudo reassured her cousin as she held back tears. "We will find a way to get Mbuya the best possible treatment."

Rudo tiptoed back into the meatpacking plant, taking long, drawn-out, deep breaths to soothe herself. Her phone was back on silent, the vibration switched off this time, carefully tucked in her pocket, under the apron where no one could see it. She wore her bravest face, hoping to slip back into work without being noticed.

"You are stepping out again when it's not your break," Mr. Jones, her heavyset white supervisor with a bald head and gray beard, admonished her. "You know there are many immigrants waiting for this job? You're asking to be fired, Rudo." His potbelly had outgrown his shirt, leaving his lower abdomen exposed and dangling in front of his thighs. Rudo apologized profusely, but he simply shook his head and walked away. He was right; this was one of the few meatpacking plants that would hire immigrants without checking their papers. So many would gladly replace her if she was fired. She wanted to explain that her Mbuya was dying, but she knew Mr. Jones had traded his heart in when he took this job. She closed her eyes and imagined him as one of the freshly butchered pigs hanging above her.

When her paycheck came, she'd been docked twenty hours of work. She knew it was punishment for stepping out for the call.

But it lasted no more than five minutes. It was unjust for him to withhold so much pay, and this wasn't the first time it had happened. The last time her paycheck was missing twenty-five hours of work, he said it was because she had shown up late all week. She'd had a flat tire and had to take public transportation. The closest bus dropped her off ten minutes from the plant, and she had to walk the remainder of the way, the wicked sun taunting with every step she took. It had taken her a week to get the tire replaced. She begged one of her babysitting families for an advance to buy a replacement. During that week, she also lost income from driving for Uber. She should have known better than to step out before her break. Now she would not be able to send her parents their monthly housing stipend, only their four-hundred-dollar grocery allowance. She knew Baba would be disappointed in her. He would remind her how all the other parents with children in America had brand new homes. He would recite scripture on the importance of honoring one's parents. He would remind her of how hard he had worked at the mine so she could have an education, that she owed him, and now that she was educated, she was abandoning her roots.

Each time, Rudo wanted to tell him that she was no more educated than she was when she left Zimbabwe twelve years ago. Yes, she had received a full scholarship to study whatever she wanted, but after she failed to make the 3.0-grade point average that first semester, she lost her funding. She could not afford to return for the second semester and pay fifteen thousand dollars out of pocket. This was a prerequisite to reclaiming her scholarship, so she never returned to college.

It was not because she didn't study hard. All night, she dipped her feet in a bucket of ice to keep her from falling asleep to review the material from classes she'd missed. But during that first semester in 2008, Zimbabwe's economy had begun to spiral, and galloping inflation made it impossible for her family to fend for themselves. Rudo picked up more hours at her campus job and even found work at a nearby farm, picking berries in season.

She sent all her earnings to her parents, who, in turn, paid tuition for her three younger siblings and fed her older brother, his wife and kids, and her cousins. They would've all starved had she not worked those extra hours. But working forty hours a week on top of a full course load while navigating culture shock took its toll, and she ended the semester with four B's and a C, and it was that C that cost her her future. She often replayed the final exam in her head, wondering what would've come of her life had she picked A instead of D for question five or C instead of B on question twenty.

She never told anyone in Zimbabwe that she had dropped out of school, thereby losing her F-1 status. After four years in the US, she borrowed a graduation gown and sent pictures to her family, lying that she was done with college. She hoped to make them proud, but this precipitated larger requests. As parents with a child in America, they could no longer be maroja – renters. She was to buy them land and send them four hundred dollars a month for the building fund. With each month of scraping off dandruff from strangers' heads, wiping mucus off the faces of strangers' babies, and ferrying rude strangers who vomited in her car after drinking too much, she added to the structure, now at window level.

Her younger brother, Lovemore, wanted to go to university in South Africa after completing his A-Levels. Rudo was expected to pay his tuition. He was smart, a bright boy with straight A's. It was her responsibility as the successful sister to pull up the rest of her family, so she found more strangers for more dollars. During this time, she continued paying boarding school tuition for the two youngest siblings as well.

Now, working eighty hours a week, Rudo had no friends. She went to her studio apartment to sleep for four hours, if she was lucky, before heading back to the plant. There was no one to speak to, no one with whom to share the burden of caring for her relatives. Where was she to find time to make friends and socialize when she barely had time to sleep? Where would the money for socializing come from? And yet, every time her mother called, she said, "You are getting old, and it is time for you to marry and have your own family," her voice soft, concerned. "The window for women is narrow. Even your cousin Ruvimbo, who was in primary school when you left, has a two-year-old now." In her mother's tone, she heard shame and disappointment.

Each time she wanted to say, "Do you want a son-in-law or a house? A grandchild or an education for your three youngest children? You have to choose." But each time, she responded, "Yes, Amai."

How could she afford her own family when she could barely afford them? Besides, caring for all those Zimbos made her feel like she had ten children already. The idea of bringing more mouths into this world that she would be responsible for gave her nightmares.

To compensate for the withheld wages, she approached a neighbor and asked to borrow four thousand dollars, assuring him that she would have the money back to him in a month.

"Fine," he eventually hesitantly agreed. "But if you don't pay me back, I'll take your car and sell it."

In the way his nose crinkled, his eyes narrowed, and he formed gentle fists as he spoke, she knew he might take more than just her car. All night, her conscience tossed and turned; she knew she would not be able to pay him back. She had two options. She could stay in the apartment and lose her car to her creditor come the end of the month, but the loss of her car would mean the loss of transportation and income from driving for Uber. Or, she could skip out on her lease, move into her car, and use the rent money to pay her neighbor back. Did she really need an apartment? After all, she was barely home. Rudo settled on the latter. For Mbuya's treatment, it was worth it.

Within a few weeks, she received confirmation that Mbuya was on the mend. The treatment had been successful, though Rudo lived in her Toyota now. But what price can one pay for the life of their grandmother?

A text message came in as she braided a skinny Senegalese woman's head. It was Taurai, her older brother. He needed to buy a stand so he could build his family a home. The cost would be eight thousand dollars.

An exasperated moan escaped her, startling the Senegalese woman, who, in turn, dropped her glass of red wine on the oak floor. Rudo apologized, rushing to grab paper towels from the woman's kitchen counter. She got on her knees to wipe up the wine, but the woman stopped her, looked her in the eyes, and asked, "Are you ok?"

Rudo buried her face in the paper towel and wiped away the tears she'd held in for weeks. The woman rubbed her back as she heaved. Instead of proffering comfort, the touch of a human unleashed depths of sorrow she had buried in the crevices of her soul.

She got up and ran to the bathroom, distancing herself from the strange hurricane of emotions evoked by having a human ask her if she was ok, touch her to comfort her, things she hadn't experienced in years. Taking out her phone, she typed in capital letters. "I DON'T HAVE ANY MONEY!"

Almost instantaneously, a response came in.

"But you are out here building a home for our parents, sending one brother to university in SA, the others to boarding school, and yet you have done nothing for ME. I haven't asked for anything until now. You even drive a nice Corolla out there with your fancy degree but are leaving me, your family, destitute."

Normally, she would have avoided a conversation, but, fueled by rage, Rudo dialed his number on WhatsApp. He answered, puffing with frustration. She could hear the chatter of the rest of the family in the distant background as Taurai asserted that no one in the family loved or cared about him, his wife, or their kids. Rudo heard what sounded like Mbuya's voice in his background. Feeling soothed by Mbuya's voice, she gently asked Taurai if he could pass the phone to her. She must've been visiting.

"I'm so glad that you are out of the hospital, Mbuya. I was afraid, given how sick you were, that you would..." Her voice trailed off.

"What are you talking about? I was never sick or in hospital," Mbuya answered, bewildered.

Rudo heard Tinashe laugh in the background. "Anonyanya kuomera stereki. Takatotaurirana kuno kuti ndikakumbira ndirini, inobuda mari."

Her cousins had conspired to swindle her. "What are we to do with a mere hundred dollars?" Tinashe said in the background, calling her stingy for only sending them small amounts whenever they asked her for money.

Rudo discovered from her brother that they had used the money to throw a party at Lake Chivero. They butchered a cow, cooked rice, ordered drinks, and partied with friends. A symbol of status that they were living the Zimbabwean dream. They had easy access to diaspora cash, a cousin in the US who could support their lifestyles. Each relative had a list—the latest fashion, iPhones, businesses they were going to launch, all to be funded by Rudo. She hung up. Slowly, she finished braiding the Senegalese woman's hair.

She stopped at the towering cathedral for a reprieve from the Texas heat. Its large bright, stain-glass windows emitted rainbow hues in the moonlight. The church always had a sign for free canned goods. As she collected tins of green beans, peas, corn, and soup, her anger grew. This was what she was resorting to for food, yet her hard-earned money had been spent in a single day by those brutes she called cousins.

Her older brother, Taurai, stopped speaking to her. He was furious that she had refused to send him eight thousand dollars for a stand, though she had easily forked four thousand for a mere party for Tinashe. As she stepped back into the humid shadows of night, a stray black dog sat at the church door, surrounded by five puppies stepping over each other for a chance to suckle. The mother gently licked each of her puppies and wagged her tail when she noticed Rudo. If my family were dogs, they would be the kind to eat their own puppies, she thought.

Rudo had previously read that two billion US dollars were remitted back to Zimbabwe each year by those living and working in the diaspora. She wondered how much of that two billion was earned in odd jobs and overtime pay in exchange for sleep. As she lay in the back seat of her car for the night, her phone flashed on her lap.

"Your older brother's kids are not in school. You should send him five hundred dollars so he can transfer them to a private school. Government school teachers are on strike. They are not getting an education at Alfreid Beit."

She sighed. The same brother who was not speaking to her? What was she to do? Let her niece and nephew go uneducated because of their tiff? But if she started paying their tuition now, how long would she have to support them? Would she have to take them through university? Even if Taurai or her parents didn't ask her to fund their university education, she was certain her niece would ask once she was old enough. At four years old, she'd already learned that Rudo was the mwena you harvested ishwa from. "Aunt Rudo, when you return, buy me a fire truck with *real* people in it," she had asked.

It was going to be harder now that she was living in her car. She couldn't transport passengers for Uber, but perhaps she could deliver for Doordash or UberEats instead? Rudo drove as far from her apartment as she could go without being too far from her primary job at the meat plant. She was determined that her neighbor would never find her to ask for his money back or to lay claim to her car. She had never been a dishonest person, and the weight of guilt settled in her lungs.

"By the way, they're pregnant again, expecting twins this time!

Be sure to send them money for a gift to welcome the babies and for baby preparation," her mother texted.

"How about I gift them birth control!" she said to herself out loud. She knew it was not because they had no access to it, though. Her older brother had always said he wanted a big family. This was an intentional addition.

Rudo parked two blocks away from the meat plant. Looking around the dimly lit parking lot, she decided this would make a decent stop until she could afford her own place again. Every night thereafter, she would return to this lot, with its tall leafy trees that cast shadows into the already dark night. There was not a person in sight. There would be no one to report her to authorities. She wondered where her cousin Tinashe was sleeping. What did his room look like? How comfortable was his bed? She opened her Facebook and scrolled through the pictures of Tinashe's party. Strangers with raised glasses, making toasts, grilling meat, and dancing her money away. The caption, a brag: "Haunawo chikwambo chako chiri mhiri?" and on another, "Tisu mbinga dzacho."

Perhaps it was time to tell them that she never did graduate, that she lived in her car and worked four odd jobs, but that would mean admitting she had been living a lie for over a decade. What would her father say? What a disgrace she would become to the family. The world would know that she was the one who received a full scholarship but made nothing of the opportunity.

An article on her Facebook feed posted by a high school friend caught her eye: "Increased suicide rates among Zimbabweans living abroad." Rudo closed the app and decided to send a text message to her supervisor to inquire about the missing hours from her last paycheck. She clenched her teeth and awaited a response.

"I'm sick of your tardiness. Don't return tomorrow. I'll find a replacement," read the response. The words in the text message picked up her fighting spirit and pinned it to the windshield.

Rudo buried her head in her lap and sobbed. She glanced at the message one more time, contemplating how to respond. Instead, she opened the Google app, paused, then slowly typed, "How to end your life."

If she made it look like an accident. Her family would never know.

An Ostrich Partnership

There he is, knee-deep in mud, a shovel in one hand and a book about weeds in the other. In his mouth is a bag of seeds. He lifts the hand with the shovel to his face and wipes the condensation off his glasses with his wrist, leaving specs of dirt on the lenses. He mumbles something to himself, and, in the process, he drops the bag of seeds he was clutching in his teeth, scattering seeds all over the raised bed. He loses his balance attempting to save them.

A squirrel stands at a distance, tempted by the plunder. Tawanda notices it right away and rushes to shoo it away. He is already at war with the squirrels, having set traps across the yard, complete with motion sensors that wake him in the middle of the night in case of an intrusion. The corn is covered with a net that he tried to chew on himself just to validate what the store associate promised—squirrels can't chew through it. The only reason he hasn't tried poisoning them is that he's afraid it might linger in the yard, and when our baby, who is not yet born, is of crawling age, she might accidentally eat some.

My husband has never grown a thing in his life, but since I mentioned a craving for freshly-harvested boiled peanuts in passing, he has made it his mission to turn our Boston backyard into a Zimbabwean botanical garden, complete with contingencies for any other craving that might arise during my pregnancy.

My phone rings, barely a few steps away from where I lie. He shouts for me not to get up; he will grab it. I shake my head as he first chases the squirrel away, then washes his hands at the outdoor sink. By the time he gets to the phone, we've missed the call. I'm a little annoyed. A text message comes in shortly thereafter.

"My mom is at your folk's place. We missed their WhatsApp call. Are you up for this?" he asks, rolling his eyes.

"It's fine. They mean well, babe," I respond.

He sighs and presses the button to return the call, planting a kiss on my forehead and gently rubbing my belly.

"Nhai baba vangu Mbizi, ungati kufuta kwemuroora here uku? How are you *this* fat, my daughter? Are you sure you're not carrying twins?" his mother says as she puffs out her cheeks as soon as she answers the call.

I laugh, swallowing my insecurities. Tawanda, who holds the phone up for me, is not in the camera view. He shakes his head and whispers to me that I'm beautiful.

"What are you feeding her? Are you avoiding eggs and lemons?" his mom starts with her superstitions. I hear my grandmother's voice in the background and smile at the thought that my baby will make four generations of Mudimu women.

"Have you decided on her name yet?" his mom jumps in. "Please name her Clara, after Tawanda's sister, who died as a child."

Tawanda feels for his mother. The only daughter she birthed died from measles because of a lack of access to vaccines. He wants to honor his mother's struggle and provide reprieve for her pain, but it's important to me that our children have Shona names. He wants me to consider Clara as a middle name, but I'm superstitious about naming my baby after a child who didn't live long. We've stopped discussing names. He doesn't understand my obsession with Shona names. He reminds me that our parents, grandparents, and even great-grandparents were all given English names. I tell him that it's because having an English name is one of the few things belonging to the white man that wasn't outlawed in the colonial days. I understand why they chose English names, especially given how people in America struggle with my name. Now imagine living in a country colonized by the British where segregation is all you've ever known.

"Saka achasungirwa here?" my grandmother asks.

Tawanda's eyes grow large. He mouths, "H to the NEVER!" as he waves his finger dramatically in the air. I try to hold in the laughter. Kusungirwa is a custom where a soon-to-be first-time mother is sent back to her parent's home to give birth. The idea is to provide loving maternal support in the month leading up to the birth as well as the first few months after birth. The soon-to-be father doesn't come with his wife, but word is sent to him to come and visit once the baby is born. Fathers are not expected to know the first thing about babies. I don't blame my family for thinking this way, watching the animal kingdom, lions lazing around while waiting for the lionesses to hunt all day and serve dinner. Most primate dads have nothing to do with caring for their young, and don't get me started on all the other species that eat their young if they stumble into Dad's territory. Having your mother's support to prepare and recover without having to cater to a grown man is the loving thing to do. My mother did it, his mother did it, and my grandmother did it. I always imagined my mother by my side when I went into labor, especially given that she's a midwife. She would dote over me if she were here now, over the baby and me after she's born, and with her as the expert, Tawanda would feel useless in her presence.

"We decided that if you don't come to give birth here, then Mai Tawa and I will take turns coming there to help you," my mother says as she gestures to Tawanda's mom. "I can be there for the first six months, and when I leave, she will come. That way, you have help for an entire year."

I want my mother here for six months, I want her to deliver her grandchild, but I don't want six months with *his* mother. I'm not sure how to tell my mother-in-law that or how to tell Tawanda. Last week when I wished my mother was around to comfort me, he walked around sulking all day, feeling like he wasn't enough for me. I understand Tawanda's argument for not wanting my mother here for that long. We'll be learning how to function as a new family unit and need room to establish our own rules without interference. Often, I want to tell him that he has our mothers confused, that his would interfere and establish rules all over the place—mine wouldn't.

"We're still figuring out the logistics," Tawanda responds quickly. Since Zimbabwe grants one-year visas, he's decided to apply for their visas but wait until two months before they expire before we fly them over. That way, we are not the ones kicking them out; we can blame the government. According to his plan, each will have a month with us but only when the baby is at least six months old. Can't I have *both* my mother and my husband?

After we hang up, Tawanda shakes his head. "Are we sure we want them here even for four *weeks*?"

I bite my lower lip. I'm going to have to shutter his plan.

Because Tawanda is a software developer and has led multiple engineering teams over the years, he has commissioned a freelancer to build baby games in Shona for our unborn child. He even found a tutor who gives Shona lessons over zoom because I mentioned how important it was for me for our child to speak our language. He's obsessed with real estate in Harare and believes we should spend a lot of summers at home so she can have an immersive experience. Over the top, I know, but who am I to stop him? He says this is why he went through all those hard years as a new immigrant.

"What else am I going to do with the money?" he says.

I can think of a lot of other things he could do with the money. Besides, if my mother were here for as long as I want her to be, the baby could have a fully immersive Shona experience from birth. But let him be—he's headstrong, especially about his unborn daughter.

I often think about how we'll raise her; daydream about our baby having the luxury to do what she loves, not what she *has* to do to survive. Not only will our baby have an inheritance, but she will never have to carry the burden of providing for her parents or, worse still, for her younger siblings should we choose to have more children. This is a burden Tawanda and I both understand all too well.

He sprawls on the couch next to me and scrolls through his apps. Lately, he has taken to watching YouTube videos. First, it was *How to Make Virgin Mango Margaritas and Mai Tais*. He gave up drinking during the pregnancy, despite my insistence that only one of us had to suffer. I told him that he could still drink and give me tasting notes, but he insisted. Then he learned how to give foot and lower back massages because I mentioned that those areas hurt. Boxes show up on our doorstep every other day—humidifiers, pacifiers, baby bottles, and so much more. But nothing is ever good enough. He watches product reviews on all things baby. Tawanda is obsessed with corners, electrical plugs, and he has even created his own "toy danger index." We didn't have any of this growing up, yet we were just fine. I worry he will be a helicopter parent, while I have dreams of letting her loose to roam the streets of Sakubva, where my grandmother lives, unsupervised, like I used to do. I dream of dropping her off at my parents' house in Zimbabwe for three weeks so she can play with her cousins while we vacation in Rome. My parents dropped me off at my grandma's for weeks on end during the school holidays, and, during this time, I formed the strongest bonds with my cousins. That's why we're best friends to this day.

"I hope she looks just like you - kasponono. The world would be a better place with more of you in it," he often says.

I joke that because the nanny we hired is white, people are likely going to assume that she is the adoptive mother of our baby and I'm the maid. It worries me sometimes. Will that teach my child to be ashamed of her skin? He wants to secure a night nurse because I'm always impressed by working moms who are up all night and yet need to be in tiptop shape bright and early in leadership roles. As CEO of my e-commerce business, selling designer African clothing, I'm fortunate enough to not only have help but to work from home. My company employs almost a hundred people, all working remotely. Besides, I haven't told him that we don't need all those people because my mother *will* be here for six months.

There was a time when I lost all faith in relationships and in men. More specifically, in Zimbabwean men. I remember going on a safari at Bushman's Rock just outside of Harare with my relatives a few years ago. As we drove past a nesting ostrich, the tour guide remarked that the male ostrich, identifiable because the males are mostly black with a little bit of white on the wings, was on incubation duty, even though it was daylight. He explained that male and female ostriches take equal turns incubating their eggs. The male tends to be on duty at night because he can blend in with the night more, making him less visible to potential predators. While off incubating duty, he finds food during the day and brings it back to the hen. I remember laughing at the idea of such an arrangement existing in the animal kingdom and joked that if I ever got pregnant, I'd need an ostrich partnership.

Perhaps I simply hadn't seen enough good examples and assumed that eventually, once they marry you, they would treat you as discardable. Just look at my grandparents, his parents—most of our extended family. Yet Tawanda manages to be everything I've ever dreamed of and more in holding up his side of the partnership. The worst of my worries is his hyper involvement in caring for me, for our child. Sure, he's hesitant about having my mother here for an extended time, but if he truly understood that this is what would ultimately make me happy, put me at ease, and make this transition easier, he would come around. I look at him and smile, then laugh at myself. How did I get so lucky? Being married to the sweetest soul, who makes me laugh, makes me feel safe, protected, and thankful. And because of his sacrifices and hard work, even before I came into his life, I get to raise our little black girl with more wealth than the average American.

And all this because we both took a chance, left our homes, and leaped into the unknown in search of the American dream.

"Wakandidyisei nhai?" he says as he stares at me, caressing my face.

I laugh. "I'm the one bewitched in love, not you," I respond.

From The Author

In July 2019, I saw a clip of a primarily white crowd chanting "send her back" to congresswoman Ilhan Omar at a US President's rally. It was a tense time in US politics. And as a black woman, also an African immigrant, I remember feeling defeated, hopeless, and even hated, despite being a permanent resident and an accomplished immigrant contributing meaningfully to society.

Later that year (November), I became so overwhelmed with my life that I decided to quit my job and buy a one-way ticket to Cape Town, South Africa. At the time, I don't think I realized the impact the political climate had on me. I blamed my "stressed state" only on my job. From Cape Town, I went home to Zimbabwe for over a month before spending a few more months traveling around the world, only one-way tickets at a time.

During this break, I wrote most of the stories in this collection. How does a pharmacist end up as an author? To process, I suppose. I've always had an interest in writing, and even while in pharmacy school, I took creative writing courses. Before quitting my job, I was a member of the San Francisco Writer's Workshop, sharing my work weekly and receiving feedback from fellow writers, some accomplished, others budding. At the time, I had no expectation of ever publishing my work; writing was purely a hobby.

I realize that most of the stories written during my break are heartbreaking, harrowing, and hopeless. As I found more balance in my life, my stories and characters became happier and stronger. Some of my defeated characters also began to rebel and rise, picking up the pieces from the scenes where I left them, for example, curled up in a ball on the floor, crying, demanding alternative endings. The result is a beautiful collection of the human experience. In this collection, you will meet black immigrant women in varying circumstances. Some stories will fill you with joy, make you laugh, and cheer in triumph; others might make you hurt and cry. I'm proud of the work I put into crafting this collection, and I hope it moves you to empathize with those different from you. For immigrants, for women, for people of color, I hope you feel seen in this collection.

I'm back in Northern California, working in a role I enjoy at a pharmacy start-up in Silicon Valley. I'm stronger, healthier, and happier and continue to take writing classes to improve my craft. My passion for amplifying underrepresented voices has only grown, and I'm working with Mukana Press to bring more marginalized voices to your coffee tables and nightstands.

I hope you enjoy my work. If you do, would you consider sharing the title on your social media accounts or asking your local library to carry a copy? And if you have the means, perhaps buy a copy for a friend or family member, too.

CPSIA information can be obtained
at www.ICGtesting.com
Printed in the USA
BVHW050956240722
642826BV00005B/10/J